RagTimeBone

RagTimeBone

LYNNETTE D'ANNA

New Star Books
Vancouver
1994

Cover concept and photograph by Chick Rice
Cover design by Val Speidel
Author photograph by E. Bradley Friesen
Printed and bound in Canada by Best Gagné Book Manufacturers
1 2 3 4 5 98 97 96 95 94
First printing, April 1994

Publication of this book is made possible by grants from the Canada Council, the Department of Heritage Book Publishing Industry Development Program, and the Cultural Services Branch, Province of British Columbia

New Star Books Ltd.
2504 York Avenue
Vancouver, B.C.
V6K 1E3

Canadian Cataloguing in Publication Data
D'anna, Lynnette, 1955 —
Ragtimebone

ISBN 0-921586-37-X

1.Title.
PS8557.A56R3 1994 C813'.54 C94-910278-4
PR9199.3.D36R3 1994

dedicated to Nemah
& all my little Obsessions

in being D'anna

1

KTL stares out the window where there is Real World life.

Things, people. *Out there.*

Inside KTL's head it is all very busy, a hub of activity. Endless comings and goings.

But in her soul, it is very very still. KTL has put away feelings, making space for all that other noise.

Inside, a man shouts.

Shouting is mimicked *out there,* through her Real World windows. Man. Fist raised and shaking, his mouth shuts and gapes like some fish. Eyes bug out in the dirty-water-air of Real World which surrounds him and protects his anger. Down the street, Real World child cowers in a brown brick doorway.

Inside KTL's busy brain is a loud place to be. Everything in there moving of its own accord, at its own whim.

Presses her hand to the side of her head and kneads there with her fingertips. Like a kitten nursing at her own head, seeking some nipple solace.

Daddy, young and handsome, broad white smile, touches baby in her sleep.

Baby, restless, murmurs.

Hush sweet Princess, he croons. *Never mind, your Daddy's here.*

2

Pearce never cries. As a baby, she is perfect. The most perfect baby.

Capable hands keep her clean, but nothing warms her.

Her grandmother closes her Elm Street house door to the outside. Curious folks who come to see the new baby are kept shivering on the stoop, and they soon stop.

Pearce becomes a toddler who never laughs.

Her world expands gradually. It spills out into the yard, to its grass and trees, to the glider swing with its rusty, groaning bolts and flaking paint, the birds that shrill, and an occasional stray cat or dog or squirrel.

When she turns four, Manma takes her to nursery school, leaves her there with the other kids. Squawking, squabbling, hitting, biting. They ignore Pearce who stares at them with huge grey eyes.

Manma picks her up and together they walk back to the big, old, only-for-two Elm Street house. Sometimes they stop at the market to buy fruit or milk or greens.

"How are you ladies today?" the grocer always asks, but Manma only purses her lips and pays silently.

Pearce finally opens her mouth to talk in kindergarten.

"Please show me how to tie my shoe," she asks her teacher, with voice clear as crystal.

Her delighted teacher laughs and Pearce blinks her storm grey eyes.

"Did I speak wrong?" she asks. "Will you show me how to shoe-tie please?"

"You spoke right," says teacher. "Can you say my name?"

"You are Reimer."

"*Miss* Reimer," says the teacher. "Of course I'll show you how to tie your shoes."

They spend a while tying and untying, and then Miss Reimer walks the child home to Elm Street.

"You stop here," says the child firmly at the gate. "Manma says we don't invite strangers in."

"But I'm no stranger," the teacher says.

"You may stop here," repeats the child. "This house is only-for-two. Manma and me. Us two."

"It's a large house for just the two of you," observes teacher.

"Never-the-less," says Pearce firmly. "Thank you for the tying lesson."

In kindergarten, Pearce learns to tie, and she speaks. Once she starts talking, she can't be shut up. All those saved-up words pour out of her like lava. Her closed world opens with words.

In this town there are housewives and spinsters and widows, and there are *girls.*

Then there are the men and the boys.

Sage's mother Lorraine works at the Town Hall. Answers phones and opens envelopes for the men in charge. Wears dark tailored suits and no wife ever says she is *too sexy* to work for her husband. No one ever accuses her of being *a bimbo* or sees her filing her nails behind any desk. No one ever says she wants to be *just-like-a-man* either.

Sometimes Lorraine takes Sage to her office where she plays with rubber stamps and builds paperclip chains; she learns how to run the mimeograph.

The-girl-who-runs-this-place, the men call her mother.

Sage's daddy is a musician who works nights. During the day he washes dishes and diapers, plays hide-and-seek, cooks and cleans.

But when Sage is seven, he leaves them and he never comes back.

Sometimes he calls, says he *loves* them. Asks Lorraine for money, and she sends it. Every time.

"I'll always love him, as long as I live," she tells her daughter.

"Why did he leave?" Sage asks.

"He's a free spirit," says Lorraine.

Jerry taunts Pearce in the school playground at recess.

"You don't got no mom," he sneers.

"So?"

"You don't got no dad neither," he says.

Pearce scuffs her sneaker toe in the dirt under the swing she's on. Jerry's grinning, hung upside down from his knees on the bar beside her.

"Why aren't you playing soccer with the other boys?"

"Why don't you got a mom and dad?"

"I've got my grandma."

"My dad says she kilt them. I wouldn't live with her for all the money in the world. I'd be scairt she'd kill me too."

"My grandma never killed nobody," says Pearce, kicking dirt defiantly.

"My dad says she's a witch."

"Well she's no killer."

"Where are they then?"

"What happened to my mom and dad?" she asks Manma at the supper table that evening.

Manma stands up suddenly, gets busy at the stove.

"Jerry says his dad says you killed them," Pearce says. "But I told him!"

Manma still says nothing.

Pearce spears macaroni noodles onto her fork, shoves it in her mouth.

"You didn't, did you?" she asks.

"Don't speak with a mouthful," says her grandma sternly. "Jerry who?"

"Dreider."

"Ah," says Manma, pulling out her chair to sit. "That'd be Joe Dreider."

"Jerry."

"His father is Joe."

"Why do I live here with you?"

"Your mother got sick," says Manma. "Someone had to take you."

"Where is she now?"

"I can't say."

"What about my dad?"

Manma sucks in her lip. "Your mother got herself in trouble," she says, her voice hard.

"Oh," says Pearce. She works through the macaroni on her plate. Then she sets down her fork. "I'm not very hungry. May I please be excused?"

Her grandmother nods at the pepper mill and Pearce bolts.

On good-air days, KTL remembers a lifetimes-ago baby. Mama's cold eyes.

He was all mine before you came along.

A wind started up inside her brain, and then a blizzard inside her womb from where she grew that baby by herself.

There's my Princess.

KTL remembers.

But then up comes the wind in thickening blankets, smothering her again.

That wind howls around the bricks in KTL's brain.

3

In summer Lorraine keeps a garden. The garden gives them food like pickles, jams, preserves, and fresh-frozen vegetables all winter.

In winter she shovels walks and driveways, even for their neighbours.

She sews their blankets from old scraps, and clothes for Sage from scratch.

On weekends she bakes and cooks. Hot fluffy buns and breads, cookies and cakes. Homemade egg noodles in chicken broth, meat stews, and casseroles.

She does this all aside from her full-time job.

"Why don't we just buy bread?" Sage asks. "You wouldn't have to spend your whole weekend in this kitchen. You wouldn't have to be so tired all the time."

"I like to make it," says Lorraine. "Besides, what could smell better in the house than fresh-baked bread?"

"I don't mind," Sage says. "I like store-bought stuff."

"Just white glue," Lorraine sniffs. "This way I know for sure what's in it."

"If you teach me how, I could help and you could just relax sometimes."

"I want you to enjoy your childhood," Lorraine says. "I don't want you to work all the time, like I did when I was a kid."

"But I wouldn't mind," says Sage. "So what if it gets a little dusty, no one but us sees it."

Lorraine goes right on cooking and cleaning, being perfect.

Sage retreats to her own room and stares from her bed at the flat, white ceiling, hands behind her head.

She wants to paint up there.

Planets around a Sun, Sun in the centre with Earth hovering nearby. Sun a mother duck surrounded by her ducklings. Some small and close, under her skirts, some more independent and further away. Wanderers like Jupiter, Saturn, Neptune.

She asked, but her mother said *no*.

"How would we ever cover those dark colours? It would use far too much paint," she said.

"I bet Daddy would let me," said Sage.

"Out of the question, young lady," her mother said.

She can hear her outside now, chatting to old Mrs. Schultz next door.

She will get the paints herself and just do it. After it's done, what can Lorraine do about it? Maybe she won't even notice. With any luck, she won't even notice.

Sage will paint her ceiling first, then figure out how to deal with Lorraine.

"Why don't we have Christmas like everyone else?" asks Pearce.

"We don't believe in Christ in this house," says Manma.

"Did we used to?"

"Before you."

"Why not now?"

"I lost my faith," says Manma, turning away.

"Because my mother got sick?"

Manma doesn't answer.

"Can I make us a Christmas?"

"I don't believe in it," says Manma.

"Just tinsel," Pearce says.

Manma shrugs, goes back to her ironing.

So Pearce gathers greenery and branches fallen in the snow and drags them back to Elm Street. Makes decorations from odd bits of cardboard, fabric, and sparkles. Puts it all together and claps her hands. "Look!" she cries.

Manma looks grim.

"Isn't this nice?"

"Not to me."

"Maybe I could tell my mother," Pearce suggests. "She's not still sick, is she? Maybe I could find her and get her to come here for Christmas."

"I don't think so," Manma says. "Anyway, how would you find her?"

"Don't you even know where she is?"

"I think of her as dead," says Manma.

Pearce tries to imagine her head on someone's shoulder, a soft whisper.

I love you.

Manma never once says it. And Pearce never asks.

She tugs down all her sparkles and branches, and tosses them helter-skelter in the big garbage bin behind Grandma's house.

I love you, *love you little Princess.*

No! she says loudly, but inside. *Please Jesus,* she prays, *just let me go.*

4

Pearce can climb any tree higher than any boy and she can scale any fence. Sage clings to her like some stubborn shadow. The other kids call her *dyke*.

"Who gives?" sneers Pearce.

Sage doesn't *give*, but she breaks Danny Stevens' finger over that word.

"Say UNCLE," she screams into his little scared face. "You say UNCLE or I'll crack your stupid head open!"

"Uh-uh-uncle," stammers Danny, but it's too late for him.

Sage has bent his finger so far back that it just dangles there, useless.

"That'll teach you," she hisses. "Don't you ever say that about my friend again. I'll kill you, I swear it. I'll hunt you down and break every fucking bone in your body."

Pearce giggles when she finds out what Sage did to Danny's finger. Twists her arm inside Sage's elbow and laughs.

"You're the best bodyguard ever," she tells her.

Pearce's mother went away a long time ago.

"Because she got sick," Pearce says. "But someday I'm gonna find her. When I'm a famous writer and travel around the world, there she'll be."

"How will you know who she is if you do find her?" asks Sage.

"I just will."

"What about your dad?"

"I don't have any dad."

"I thought you needed a dad to be made."

"You don't really need one. You don't need one for anything, really."

"For the, you know, the sperm part," Sage says. "The fucking part."

"Oh, any old guy would do for that," says Pearce airily.

"Do you know who's your dad?"

"All I know's she had to give me to Manma."

"You need some real girlfriends," Lorraine says, thumping the bread dough smooth.

"Other girls are boring," says Sage, poking her finger into the elastic ball and watching the dough spring back. "All they do is talk about make-up and boys. They don't even *think* about anything else."

"Get away from my dough," Lorraine says, swatting at the air by her daughter's hand. "It just looks a little odd. Hanging around with this tomboy who doesn't seem to know if she's a girl or a boy."

"Pearce and me think about lots of different stuff," says Sage, sucking dough off her finger. "And what looks so odd about friends?"

"She doesn't even know who she is."

Sage leans on her elbows, watching her mother split the ball into loaves. "How does that make her a bad friend?"

Lorraine shrugs.

"Did you ever know Pearce's mother?" Sage asks suddenly.

Lorraine plops loaves into greased pans, wraps them under a clean striped dish towel.

"What do you know about Pearce's mother?"

"Just that she got sick and gave her baby away. Pearce plans to find her someday."

"Well," says Lorraine, checking the kitchen wall clock. "I suppose I'll wash these bowls now, so I don't have to do them later."

"She doesn't even know who her dad was," Sage says. "At least I got to know Daddy."

"Everyone's got something," Lorraine says absently. "Some little secret."

"What's yours?"

"Except me. What you see is who I am."

Sage sighs.

"Sometimes I miss Daddy so much," she says softly. "Don't you?"

The old house belongs to Manma. When she dies, not that she ever will being as stingy as she is, this Elm Street house will go to Pearce. She buys only what they need to get by. Nothing extra. No television, no stereo, no special clothes, and she stores her savings in a tin which she keeps hidden away.

Once Pearce spies her combing through a ragged chocolates box.

She pounces. "Are those pictures?" she asks. "Let me see."

Manma's hard hand covers the box. "No!" she says.

"Who's this guy?" asks Pearce, tugging at paper through the cracks between her fingers.

Suddenly Manma lets go and Pearce is holding a photograph of a sneering man slouched against a shiny red convertible.

"Who is he?" she demands.

Manma stares in a silence that stretches long and thin as a cracking ice river. Then air leaks from her mouth. "You can take it," she says finally. "It makes no difference."

Later, Pearce examines that photo face, but there's nothing in it she can recognize.

"I think that church kicked her out because my mom got in trouble," she tells Sage. "I think that's why she got so mean."

"How could that be her fault?"

"When children sin, they say it's the parents' fault. Ask your mother."

"Everything is sin," says Lorraine. "Me with your father, that was sin too."

"What was wrong with Daddy?"

"He didn't go to church. He was in a jazz band. I wasn't pregnant when I married him, but I might as well have been. They kicked me out."

"What about your parents?"

"They stayed with the church," says Lorraine. She twists her wedding band off her ring finger, holds it up between her fingers to the lamplight. "Them and their church."

"Why didn't they get kicked out too?"

"They disowned me," Lorraine says, dropping the band on the coffee table. "I wasn't even allowed at their funerals."

Princess waits for Daddy in the hall after work. Mama in the kitchen, Daddy in the hall.

Big kiss for Daddy. Big kiss from Daddy's little girl.

How's my little Princess? he asks every day like clockwork.

Waiting for you, Daddy, she says, the same.

Rush of wind, sudden rush of wind blows Daddy against her. Inside, inside her brain.

He laughs, pulls back, looks around.

Mama's in the kitchen, making supper. Spaghetti, we will eat spaghetti today, she sings louder than the wind between them.

Making Daddy happy is all, is all. Is all.

5

Rita's three brothers are both ahead of her and behind her. She's smack in the middle of all those disgusting boys.

When she was small, Raymond was already there. He was first and he knows it.

"I'm the best," he brags all the time. Bigger means better to a boy, she finds out soon enough. Any old thing Raymond wants to do, Raymond can do. Every time Rita wants to do something, it's the third degree.

First Raymond, then Rita, then Danny, and finally Timmy.

"Don't you wish he was a girl?" she asks her mother after Timmy.

Mother says *no.*

"Why not?"

"Girls are too much bother," her mother says.

Rita isn't. Not compared to Raymond. Not even to Danny. And way less than baby Timmy.

"Bother how?"

"It's hard to raise a girl right. They get themselves into trouble and you never live it down."

"What kind of trouble?" she persists.

Imagines a car wreck on a highway, all twisted and grotesque, with blood pouring like ketchup all around. But in Rita's mind, it's boys behind the steering wheel. Girls, if any, are only passengers.

"Girls have to get married," says her mother.

"Boys get married too."

"The girl's parents have to pay."

She passes Rita the empty diaper pail. Now there are twenty-four white cotton squares flapping on the outside washline. Some shit-stained forever, by now on their fourth baby.

Rita dawdles over the pail.

"Take the pail."

"I will," she says, "but I'd like you to explain."

"When you're older, you'll understand."

"When I'm older, will you tell me?"

Picks up the pail and swings it so it cracks against her kneecap. Looks up at her big, sad mother.

"Maybe," mother answers.

Her mother is busy with a family to raise, and a husband with a shoe store and a mistress.

Snooping through her father's desk one night, Rita finds a box of private photographs. Curiosity and guilt make her heart beat so fast and loud she can feel it in her toenails. But that doesn't keep her from looking.

The woman has a sulky face and bare naked body. Breasts with dark nipples, a round belly, and pubic hair shaped like a valentine.

Rita looks and looks, she can't stop looking at the naked body in those pictures.

What if her mother would see? Her mother's belly is a crisscross road map from where her babies were cut out, her breasts are small and saggy from where all those babies, including Rita, suckled, her knees are wrinkled and old-looking.

Rita doesn't know for sure what she looks like *down there,* but she is pretty sure there is not any heart-shaped pubic hair. Her mother does not varnish her finger and toenails red, and her hair is just plain mousy.

Silks and satins are for this platinum photo-woman.

Rita's mother chain-smokes Sweet Caporals and her finger skin is tinged sepia where she holds them.

The photo-woman's hands are like some ad for hand cream, and her eyes are languid.

Mother's eyes look baggy and bloodshot most of the time from too little sleep, too many kids, and the Valium her doctor gives her to *keep her calm.*

Rita tucks the photo-woman safely back inside her box, puts that box carefully back inside her father's drawer. The exact same pile of things in the exact same order as before.

Afterwards, whenever she looks at him, she thinks of the photo-woman in his drawer.

She stares and stares at herself naked. Pulls her kid-belly tight, moulds her flat breast flesh together to make cleavage, and pretends.

No one *real* has any energy left.

Hippie girls had babies and had to grow up.

Drugs, sex, and rock'n'roll are still a boy's game.

Rita wants to leave her hair a scraggy mass, to slop around in ripped bellbottoms.

Wear love beads and go to Woodstock.

Do acid in the rain.

Go to love-ins.

But she's too late.

With those three brothers, survival is a cut-throat business.

The younger ones are easier for her to control as long as Raymond isn't around. Raymond threatens to break her fingers, threatens to smash in her head, or to paralyze her. He's always practising some stupid Kung Fu move. But mostly he picks fights with Danny, which keeps Rita out of it and keeps Raymond busy.

She does her jobs around her mother's house and hides inside her books when she can. When the housework is done. Otherwise she keeps busy and away from that house.

When her father is home, he sits in front of the television in the rumpus room. Watches sports and sitcoms, and chews gum.

He isn't really there even when his body fills the black leather recliner.

"Do you love Daddy?" Rita asks her mother one afternoon while they are doing dishes.

Her mother looks vague and says nothing. Pauses in her pot-washing to pick at some dried-on macaroni with a broken white fingernail.

"Well, do you?" Rita insists, grabbing at the plate her mother has perched precariously on the drain board.

"I suppose," her mother finally says.

"Does he love you?" Rita asks, searching for some thread to sew together her tangled thoughts.

Mother stands with her wrinkled, broken hands in the scummy dishwater, and stares out through the window over the sink. Danny and Raymond are playing soccer in the field behind their garden. Little Timmy is still napping in the bedroom, too young to play anyway.

"We're married," she says, her words followed by a loud period. "You finish these pots, I'm going to rest before Timmy wakes up."

She dries her hands on the apron hanging on the cupboard door beside the sink.

Rita looks out at the brothers through the window. Fists are flailing. Raymond is on top.

She sinks her hands into the dishwater, swishes them round and around.

In the dishwater she sees a reflection of her father's photo-woman.

She jerks at the plug and the water spirals down the drain with a loud slurping noise. The photo-woman a genie in reverse.

When Rita follows along behind her brother, the teachers think they have her pegged and she is forced to prove to each one that she is no Raymond.

Prove that although they are both on the same planet at the same time, and in the same family, anything beyond is meaningless.

Rita shows them.

In small towns, this is the way it is, no getting around it. *You are your family.*

In this town you can't hide from your makings.

6

Sometimes she pretends her mother is a dragon-slayer, invincible, fighting off dragons with her brave and flaming sword. But it's not working because stiff-word dragons stalk Pearce anyway: *Selfish & Ungrateful, Envious & Greedy.* Always *Angry*.

Someday she will find that dragon-slayer-mother, young and beautiful. Still younger and more beautiful than Pearce can ever be.

I've had to make my own way, Pearce will tell her then. *I faced the dragons myself, no thanks to you. And you,* she will ask, *where have you been, hiding away all this time?*

Pearce will be the fiercest dragon-slayer of them all. She will be the Dragon-Slayer Queen.

Sage is doing homework and Lorraine is taking down the hem on a skirt. The news is on television.

Sage answers the phone on the first ring. "Oh, it's you. Yeah, she's here, just a minute." She covers the mouthpiece. "It's Daddy," she says.

Lorraine drops the skirt, reaches eagerly for the telephone.

"He probably wants money again," says Sage. "Don't give it to him."

"Hi," Lorraine says brightly.

Sage mutters, picks up her notebook, drops it. Watching her mother's face, animated and glowing, making banking arrangements.

"Do you want to talk?" Lorraine asks her at last.

"Tell him to go fuck himself," Sage says loudly.

Her mother winces.

"She can't talk to you right now. Maybe next time."

"All he ever wants is money," says Sage after Lorraine hangs up. "That's the only reason he ever calls. He doesn't give a shit about *us*."

"He loves you."

"Where is he then? Why doesn't he ever visit? Why doesn't he ever call just to talk? Why doesn't he send stuff?"

"You see things only one way," Lorraine says quietly. "You don't see the whole picture."

"It's no use even talking to you," rages Sage. "Nothing ever changes."

Rita escapes to the laundry room in the basement to read.

Wraps herself in an old blue-toned afghan which she hides on a corner shelf dusty with cobweb soot and laundry lint; curls against the corner behind the dryer on a sofa cushion she rescued from the garbage bin and cleaned herself.

This is her own special nest where she is safe. Safe from snot-nosed brothers, safe from endless housework, safe from goofy television cartoons.

One day Raymond shoves through the door.

"There you are," he says, eying her nest.

Rita quickly closes her book, tucks it under the afghan.

"What do you want?" she asks.

"So this is where you go to hide," he smirks.

"Never mind," she snaps.

"Mom wants you to babysit the brats. Better get up there before they find you."

She's in a Nancy Drew phase, with her nose pressed firmly into one or another of the mysteries whenever she has a chance.

So the next time he creeps into the laundry room, she doesn't even notice.

Not when he stealthily shuts the door.

Not when he slides the bolt in place.

"Hey," he says softly, and she jerks to attention. "I've got something for you to read. Look at this." Smirking, he shoves his *something* into her face. "Look," he orders. *Hustler.*

Rita shrinks. Her brother is between her and the door. The magazine is between her and Nancy Drew.

"Look," he commands again. "*Girls.* All kinds of girls. You like *girls*, don't you?"

She can't help it. She looks. She has no choice. "Please don't," she says.

"Don't what?" he asks, still oddly quiet.

"Don't make me look," she pleads. She feels tears in the back of her throat, but she won't cry, not in front of *him*.

"You know what I do when I look at all these girls?" he asks.

"Please," she says again.

"This," he says, pulling at his zipper. Tugs out a protruding stiff piece of flesh.

Rita has had to diaper boys, she knows what it is. It just looks so different in Raymond's hand, so much bigger, so much more menacing. He wraps his hand around it, moves the skin back and forth, back and forth, his eyes dark.

"I'm leaving," Rita says. "I don't have to watch you do that."

"Wait," he says breathlessly. "Show me yours."

She jumps up, scattering magazine and Nancy Drew and afghan. The magazine flips pages to a woman with tacks piercing her skin.

Rita pushes past her brother crouching on the floor with his meat in his hand, fumbles with the door bolt, stomach churning.

But something else though, too. Some seed, planted deep inside: it wasn't the *women*, just Raymond with his fistful of tight flesh.

She moves her blue-toned afghan and ragged cushion seat from their hiding place in the basement. Stays as far away from her brother as she can. He's busy anyway, with a job at the shoe store and his first real girlfriend.

Lucky her, thinks Rita.

Daddy drives a red, red car, a car with wings like an aeroplane.

In this car, he says, they can *fly.*

Wind rifles through her golden princess hair when she sits beside him in the fast car. Takes her for a drive, and she screams and screams with delight.

Faster Daddy. Go faster!

Heart banging against her skull. Wind piercing through her like whistles.

Faster. Faster! she urges.

Daddy grins and grins like crazy. She laughs out loud.

Hey little Princess, you like that? he asks. *Just see how fast we can really go.*

The next thing she sees, he is holding that stiff thing between his legs inside his fist, it bounces up and down like mad.

Just watch me! he screams.

7

In the shed behind the Elm Street house, Pearce and Sage *play*. Pressing together. Locking tongues.

"Should we do this?" growls Pearce.

"It's okay," says Sage. "We're just messing around."

Pearce's stone grey eyes seek some code, some message. "Maybe we should stop," she says, pulling back.

"I want to do this," says Sage. "Really. Put your fingers *here*."

Then Pearce can't stop. Sage. Warm, warm inside her skin, and eager.

"There," says Sage urgently.

"You are so very soft," Pearce whispers.

Sage gets hot all over, very fast. "Feel how my heart is beating."

Pearce touches her breast bone gently. "Yes," she breathes.

"I'm burning up. Man, Pearce, you burn me up."

"Me too," says Pearce.

Alone in her room, Pearce drums her hands on her knees and paces the floor back and forth, forth and back.

Nearly fifteen and Sage is *only twelve* and anyway, *touching that way is not for girls.*

This house is dead silent and Pearce is on edge. Filled with jitters. Tingles from where Sage's rubbing made her sap bleed. Still wet from Sage's quicksilver tongue.

Scorched. All over, inside and out. Skin and bone.

Sage calls, lets the phone ring. Twenty times. Thirty times. This is *love*. This must be what it feels like to be *in love*.

"Who are you calling?" asks her mother. "You've dialled that phone a hundred times."

"Just Pearce," Sage says. "Her grandma's in the city and she's all alone."

"If she hasn't answered by now, she isn't going to. Don't you have homework?"

"I *have* to call. I *promised.*" Sage holds her breath, dials again, listens. "*Shit!*"

"Watch that mouth."

"Something's wrong. I have to go see."

"It's ten-thirty," says Lorraine firmly. "No time for you to be roaming the streets. That's probably what she's doing, out getting herself into trouble."

"Okay, *okay,*" says Sage, slamming down the receiver. "I'm going to bed."

She escapes through her open bedroom window, swinging easily from a tree branch to the ground.

Pearce stops her drumming, pacing.

Wanders into Manma's room. Smells like *old person.* Flannel nightgown on a hook behind the door flutters when the door swings. Pearce jumps. Catches her breath.

Slides open a bureau drawer. Mouldy underwear. Huge cotton panties with knee-length legs. *Old lady stuff.*

Rickety wooden stepladder in the basement. Pearce drags it upstairs to the end of the hallway outside her bedroom door. Underneath the attic trapdoor.

No one ever goes up there. Manma says it's empty and besides, she is *much too old to be climbing up shaky ladders.*

Shoves her head through the hole and digs around for handgrips.

Sawdust curls rain all around.

On her knees.

Downstairs, the phone rings and rings.

Boxes off in the far dark corner.

Climbs back down. Gets a flashlight. Shuffles though sawdust.

Curious terror, a pandora-second, she brushes it quickly away.

"This stuff is mine," she says aloud. "As much as anyone's."

The phone rings again. "I'm busy," she shouts.

Box top snaps up, she drops her light.

Old schoolbooks.

NAME: *Katie.*

SUBJECT: *Arithmetic.*

TEACHER: *Mr. Schmidt.*

GRADE: *Six.*

Art. Every page crammed full of childish drawing. *Open mouths, screaming.*

Another box. *Baby clothes.* Pink knitted booties with sweaters and matching bonnets.

Teeth chatter. Despite all that sawdust.

Manma comes home tomorrow.

The phone is ringing again, ring after ring after ring.

Sage finds the key underneath the mat in the sunporch.

Pearce's grandma would never allow so many lights on in her house.

She stomps into the still, bright house and up the stairs.

"Where are you?" she shouts.

"I found something," Pearce calls down through the hole in the ceiling. "Come up here."

Sage hoists herself up. "I phoned a billion times. I had to sneak out the window." She brushes at the sawdust sticking to her T-shirt.

"There's all these boxes."

"Your grandma will kill you."

"She never comes up here. And anyway, this stuff is *mine*."

Sage peers at the open boxes, the clothing, the school books.

"Why didn't she just burn these?" Pearce asks angrily.

Photographs.

Penis scratched over the face of a girl with golden ringlets; *cunt* where the head of a baby should be.

Sage swallows hard but Pearce just stands, stiff.

"Every single one. Some are of a man, maybe he's my father. They're all like this."

"You think your *grandma* did this?"

"Who the fuck else?"

"Why?"

"How would I know why?"

"What should we do?"

"Pack it all away again," Pearce kicks at the schoolbooks, "except for these."

"She'll find those in your room."

"You can keep them for me."

Together, the girls restack the boxes.

Kick sawdust back to cover the bare spots.

"I'll go down first and you pass this to me," says Pearce.

Sage curls up into a ball against Pearce's back in her bed that night. In the morning, they'll take the box to her house.

Pearce isn't sure what time Manma will return. She didn't want Sage to sleep there, but Sage insisted.

"I can't leave you here alone," she said. "Anyway, I won't really sleep. I have to get back to my own bed before Mom calls me for breakfast."

So she lies curled and half-awake, tucked into Pearce's warmth, watching the sky through the window, one hand wrapped around Pearce's breast.

"Wake up," she whispers when day begins to break.

Pearce mutters and twists the blanket up tighter around her face.

"Pearce!" Sage says loudly. "Wake up now!"

Pearce jerks awake and Sage sits up.

They hide the box in Lorraine's garage, then Pearce watches Sage climb back into her bedroom.

Wriggles out of her jeans and jumps into bed just before her mother's knock.

"Wake up, sleepyhead," says Lorraine.

"In a minute," she mumbles.

That box is tucked away inside her bedroom closet where no one but Sage will ever see it. Lorraine says her room is her own castle and it stays that way. Pearce's secret is safe.

But things change.

Pearce turns away.

Sage chases after her one day. Grabs her sleeve. "You talk to me," she demands through a faceful of angry tears. "Talk to me right now. What the hell did I ever do that you can turn me into a *Nothing*?"

Pearce turns. Dull red lips, glistening white eye powder, and the boldest black eyeliner. She doesn't even look anything like *Pearce* anymore.

"Let go of my jacket," she orders and Sage lets go. "I guess I have to tell you. I can't be your friend anymore."

"Why?"

"Because everyone says we're queer."

"So? Who cares? Not me."

"Me," says Pearce. "I'm fifteen and you're only twelve. I should know better."

Inside those black-lined eyes, Sage no longer sees herself reflected. "I'm thirteen," she retorts. "And what about your box?"

"Keep it for me."

"Why should I?"

"Because I need you to. I'll get it back later."

"When is *later* going to be?"

"You know I can't take it to Manma's," says Pearce, "and I don't have anywhere else to hide it."

"Why should I?" Sage repeats.

"Maybe for our friendship."

"What friendship?"

"Or maybe even for *love*," Pearce says.

"You don't know anything about *love*."

Pearce raises her hands, lets them drop. "I can't change this," she says then.

Sage still can't resist those smoke grey eyes.

If I have this piece, she'll have to come back, she thinks.

8

Rita starts to follow her right after she breaks up with Pearce.

Every time Sage turns around, there she is. Rita knows she's no Pearce Winthrop; she can't climb trees and she hates heights. She's scared to climb, but she adores Sage.

Sage doesn't give a shit about how she looks. Doesn't wear those cool-girl jeans. Those baby-coloured angora sweaters.

A boy's denim jacket with sleeves rolled up. Faded jeans, not store-ripped. Listens to weird music, jazz that sounds like dogs barking. Rolls her own cigarettes and smokes where anyone can see her.

Sage has no sullen father to embarrass her with his naked mistress in a drawer. Has a mother who is, everyone knows, *as-good-as-any-man*.

Rita sticks close to her for a while and finally Sage talks.

"What is it you want?" she barks. "You're like some dog in heat or something, the way you wander around behind me."

"I *like* you," Rita says bravely. "I want to be your friend."

Sage stomps her black boot hard against pavement, shakes her fist in Rita's moonstruck face. "Get lost!" she yells.

But Rita just stays there, does not shrink back, does not falter.

"I'm going to be your best friend," she says. "Your *very best friend*, if you like it or not."

"I don't need any best friend," says Sage. "And I sure as hell don't need you!"

Pearce has pulled down the blinds between them. Closed the shutters. When she passes Sage anywhere, she stares past her as though she doesn't exist.

Sage swears, smokes, and thuds around the house in heavy boots.

"What happened with Pearce?" Lorraine asks, gathering up her courage.

"Nothing," snaps Sage. Tugs strings of tobacco onto rolling paper. Scrapes a match against her jeans zipper.

Lorraine flinches. "Did you two have a fight?"

Sage draws on her freshly rolled cigarette. "She just says we can't be friends anymore. For now," she says. "She's too old for me, she thinks."

Lorraine sighs with relief and rumples her daughter's hair.

"It'll be okay, you'll see," she says.

"Yeah sure," says Sage dully. "I know."

Even though she's a girl, Rita is no extra trouble. She'll never have a wedding for anyone to have to pay for, and she's figured out the getting-into-trouble part by herself.

She works for the student newspaper, writes *Gazette* movie reviews.

Sage has a job at the theatre. She sells Rita a ticket, one, and a box of popcorn, buttered.

"Slather on the butter," says Rita.

"It'll take a minute to melt," snaps Sage, turning her back to Rita.

"Aren't you supposed to talk with your customers?" asks Rita. "Isn't there some kind of rule? Don't you at least have to be polite?"

"I don't get paid enough to be sweet. Besides, it isn't in my nature."

"But it wouldn't kill you, would it? What's the movie about?"

"Hey, I don't get to watch. I just do this."

"You never watch the movies?"

"Someone has to mind the store."

"Why don't you come in with me?" Rita asks. "We'll sit near the back and you can leave if you have to."

Sage snorts. Drizzles golden liquid over the corn, licks some off her finger.

"That's a buck seventy."

Rita waits till she puts out her palm.

Counts out her dimes slowly, touching Sage with every one.

Seventeen times she touches Sage's hand.

"Okay, you've got your pound of flesh," says Sage, closing her fist over the silver.

Opens the cash drawer, lets those dimes fall.

Watches Rita walk away, get swallowed by the theatre.

The lobby lights make a perfect screen. Sage is at its centre, counting out box office cash.

Across Main Street is the post office where Pearce slouches against the war memorial and watches.

Sage the star. Her hair falls around her eyes, head bent low in concentration.

Pearce knows every penny has to be accounted for. Accounting is Sage's most detested activity.

Pearce folds her arms across her chest, presses one warm hand around her breast, watching Sage count across the street behind the glass.

If anyone asks, she's just killing time, carving the word *fuck* into the war memorial.

These new dragons living in Pearce's body make it harder for her to fall asleep at night. She names them *Passion* and *Desire.*

Touches herself and thinks of Sage.

Thinks of Sage and can't stop.

That old woman keeps a tight watch on her. Leaves no corner of her room unturned.

"What is it you're looking for?" Pearce yells. "I need some fucking privacy!"

"Not in my house," her grandma says.

"You're not even my mother," Pearce says coldly. "Why can't you just leave me alone?"

"Never trust any man," Manma tells her for the millionth time.

"Nor any woman either," Pearce retorts. "What's left?"

"Yourself," says Manma.

"I don't even know what the fuck I am," says Pearce.

Slams the door, leaving Manma staring at her safe four walls.

She hangs out alone at night, just around.

Howie throws her out of his hotel. "You're not legal," he says. "Come back when you are."

"Aw Howie," she wheedles, "you don't even have a stripper. Just beer, big fucking deal."

"Go on, scat!" he growls.

Howie's Hotel is the oldest standing building on Main Street. People call it an *eyesore.*

Pearce slides in a second time with a doctored ID.

"Com'on, gimme a draft," she says. "I promise I won't breathe one word."

Howie winks and pours. Pearce drinks, coughs, drinks again.

Howie leans against the counter top. "You know," he says, "this is a dump. If this stinking town would give me a permit, I'd build a decent joint."

"Why won't they give you a permit?"

"They say it's sin to sell booze. I oughta burn the place down."

Pearce wipes foam from her mouth with her jacket sleeve. "The kids go to the city to drink," she says.

"So do the old guys who run this town. Half of them got mistresses on the side too."

"Who has a mistress?" asks Pearce.

Howard winks and spills another draft.

Raymond follows her down to the basement bathroom at a party.

"You've wanted me all along. I could tell," he says like a conversation.

"Get out of here," Pearce says before he traps her against the wall.

Tugs down her panties. Spreads her closed knees. Shoves his body in-between. Opens his zipper with one free hand.

"All the guys say you're a dyke," he says, excited.

"No," she protests. "Don't."

"I say they're wrong. You just ain't found the right guy to fuck with yet."

His prick leaps in his hand. Leaks against her thighs.

"What about Tina?" asks Pearce.

"Never mind about her," he mutters, concentrating. "Just wait'll you feel this."

No struggle, no victory.

She locks the door and stares back at her reflection in the mirror. Same face, same old ugly face. No point in fixing it. No one can see it anyway. All they see is what they think is there.

Scrubs herself clean with toilet paper. Scrawls chalk-white lipstick on her thick mouth. Smacks her lips and grimaces at herself.

Raymond sucks cock free, she wipes onto the mirror with her lipstick chalk.

"Tell me about my mother," she says.

"There's nothing to say," Manma says, walking away.

"Come back here!" yells Pearce. "You owe me more."

"I owe you nothing," says Manma coldly. "All my debts are paid."

Pearce can't even twitch without her noticing.

"You had a hard time getting to sleep last night," she will say. Or, "It was past two when you came in last night. Where were you all that time? What were you doing?"

"Get off my fucking back!" Pearce screams.

Manma's face crumples when Pearce yells; she wilts from the top down like an unwatered plant. But Pearce just thinks of all those *secrets.*

On the eve of her sixteenth birthday, Pearce hitchhikes to the pub in the next town. Picks up some guy and drags him back to Manma's house. They are shit-faced drunk, falling over each other.

"Let's fuck," he grunts, grabbing at her breast.

Which is when Manma appears at the top of the stairway. Her voice cracks like a whip.

"*Pearce!*"

Pearce stares defiantly. "What."

"Get rid of that person!"

"Make me!"

"You will leave this house now, young man."

"This is my fucking birthday!" Pearce shrieks. "You will not order my friends about *on my own fucking birthday*!"

"You are a bad seed," Manma says.

Pearce turns sharply.

Leaves Manma withering at the top of the stairs.

She returns to the Elm Street house one last time on her sixteenth birthday while Manma is picking up her mail at the post office. Works quickly to gather her things; helps herself to some money from the hidden banking tin.

A one-way bus ticket to the east coast will use a lot of the cash. She'll budget the rest until she finds a job.

Sticks her face inside a magazine while the bus passes the town limits.

Leaving Sage is her only sorrow. But there is nothing at all she can do about that.

Besides, she already left Sage long ago.

9

Rita follows her hero up the narrow stairs.

Afternoon sunlight paints the attic walls amber.

Sage unzips her jeans, avoiding Rita's soft bruised eyes. "Like this," she says, guiding Rita's hand.

"Wait," says Rita. Shrugs off her jacket, her denim skirt. Lifts her T-shirt over her head while Sage watches passively. "You too," she says, tugging at Sage's jacket.

Sage's body beside her on the mattress, bare underneath her shirt.

Sage positions Rita's curled hand between her thighs. Rita's fingers uncoil, lift Sage's cotton panties, gently spread the lips there. Moistens her tongue.

"Yeah," says Sage, drawing Rita's head down.

Rita presses her mouth to her lips and spreads soft kisses there. Sage is ice cream.

"*There,*" breathes Sage.

"I love you," whispers Rita easily as Pearce's birthday bus pulls out of town.

"What are you thinking?" asks Rita, idly unravelling some threads dangling from her jacket.

Sage marches on ahead, collar turned up against the biting autumn wind, head bullishly bent. Wet snow sprinkles her auburn hair and sticks there like melting dandruff.

"She's gone," Rita says. "Forget it, can't you?"

"No," snaps Sage. "Leave me alone for a change. I can't even think with you always around."

"You knew she'd go sooner or later."

"I don't need you to tell me these things. I know her better than anyone in this whole stinking town."

"Raymond bragged that he fucked her. Did you know that? You-who-knows-it-all."

Sage stops her marching. "Who says? That scum brother of yours? Is that who?"

"Yeah. So what?"

"That fucking brother of yours, he'd say anything to make a name for himself." She spits into wet snow. "Pearce never said it, did she?"

"Pearce never said anything about *anything*," Rita sneers. "She's just a secret, one great big walking secret."

Sage locks her lips, shoulders squared hard against the wind.

"She left you, didn't she?" shouts Rita. "She fucked off without even a goodbye." Kicks at frozen dirt clods with her ripped sneakers.

Sage is running now, running into that wind and away.

No *goodbye*, not one word. Rita is right. Dead right.

Pearce has gone, leaving only this empty winter air. Sage sinks deep inside it. Takes to walking long, bitter walks. But she can't freeze Pearce out no matter how much walking she does, how much cold air she breathes.

Life goes on. And on, even without *goodbyes* or warm words.

School, and work, and still everlasting Rita who manages to rub some of the chill away despite all Sage's efforts at noble loneliness.

Then she gets a postcard with a picture of a lighthouse from the east coast.

Sage tucks the lighthouse into her jeans where it keeps her warm.

Starts grinning like a crazy woman. She can't quit grinning. Grins and grins like mad.

On the coast, Pearce takes a two-room apartment with a private bath, a job typing and filing for a sales office. She opens an account with the rest of Manma's money.

The men she works for are parts salesmen; they sell car parts to car salesmen. Pearce types for them and answers their phones, files their invoices, makes photocopies and coffee, and washes up after them. She waters their office plants and cleans their toilet.

The men leave steamy little notes in their washroom for her to find when she cleans.

They want her to *be sexy*. They take her out *for drinks,* she listens to their bullshit jokes. Orders flowers for their wives after they've fucked her. *I'm sorry honey,* say their notes, *I forgot.* It's not worth the ink; a few quick thrusts and they're satisfied.

She keeps a girlfriend on the side.

Typing pays the rent, and she starts writing mystery stories. Writing and writing, trying to get it right. She sends her words to publishers who send them back.

She's left that town far behind but some kind of guilt forces her to write to Manma.

I'm doing fine, she writes.

Manma writes back once, in spider print: *Come home for a visit sometime.*

What exactly is *home*?

"This isn't really me," says Sage. "I only do this to keep you happy."

Salty pussy is on Rita's tongue. She licks it onto Sage's lips. "You taste good and I don't give a shit how you think you are, or how you think I am, I love you anyway."

"Stop saying that," Sage protests. "I'm gonna find myself a boyfriend. Everyone is talking."

"Let them. It's all they have to do. It keeps them busy."

"But I think you really are this way." She licks back at Rita's tongue.

"What if Lorraine found us up here?" asks Rita, sinking her finger inside.

Sage wriggles. "She doesn't even remember what it's for."

"Vul-va," says Rita, twisting her finger gently with each syllable. "Why won't you go down on me?"

"I keep telling you I'm not into that."

"What about with Pearce?" demands Rita.

"No," Sage lies.

"Bullshit."

Sage leans back, raising her hands above her head. Presses hard against Rita's palm. "Mmm," she hums. "Do that some more."

Eddie follows Rita all over. He's on the *Gazette* team, the Yearbook Committee, in the Drama Club. Every place she is, there's Eddie. Eager-to-please, shit-eating-grin Eddie.

"Eddie sure likes you," says Sage. "I think he wants to be your boyfriend, Rags."

"Yuck!" Rita shudders. "Poor Eddie."

"Why don't you?"

"Why don't I what?"

"Let him be your boyfriend."

Rita's lashes brush her skin like hummingbird wings.

"Why?"

"Because he wants you. He's a sweetheart."

"No. I mean *really*," says Rita, staring out the attic window. "Why?"

"I think you should try it with a guy. See what it's like. You never know, maybe you'll like it. Maybe you're not really so queer as you think you are."

"Do you really think that?"

"Who'm I to know? Guy, girl, what's the difference?"

"I have to puke just thinking about doing it with a guy."

Sage shrugs, watching the tree nod outside her attic window. Branches scrape the roof over their heads. Leaves twitch but she can't see too well. Her glasses are downstairs in her room under the planet ceiling. To her the tree is a forest green mesh.

Rags' face is in her lap, stamping fuzzy kisses onto her belly.

Eddie is Rita's best helper with the *Gazette*. She sends him on her toughest assignments and he always comes back for more. Even when he can't get what she sends him for, Eddie comes back for more.

"Remember Pearce?" she asks him one day.

"Who's that?"

"She was two grades ahead of us. She lived with her grandma, Mrs. Winthrop, on Elm Street. Her and that old lady."

"Oh yeah," he says. "She hung around with Sage."

"For a while," says Rita. "Yeah, I think so. Just for a while."

Sage holds that fucking lighthouse against the warmth of her skin. Rita has seen it, has guessed who it's from.

Pearce, who will not let Sage go, even though she is thousands of miles away. But she isn't true to her either. Wherever the wind blows her, that's where Pearce is.

Rita searches for a way to expose her.

She knocks on Pearce's grandma's door. Brave, because she tells herself she is tracking down a story. Knocks boldly on the green door.

"Hi," she says. "I'm Rita. Remember me?"

The woman looks blankly at Rita's brave mouth.

"I'm looking for Pearce."

"She doesn't live here anymore."

The woman tries to close her door but Rita butts it with her boot.

"I know that," she says quickly. "But I need her address. It's important."

The grandmother's lips are pursed. She has the crinkles around her eyes that old people get from having seen so much, lived so long.

"If you give it to me, whatever it is, I'll make sure she gets it."

"Actually, I just want to write to her. And nobody knows her address."

"If she wanted you to know it, she'd tell you."

"Well then . . . "

This woman will not let her inside. Rita can tell by the nostrils, by the tightness of face. She looks a lot like Pearce, only older. Stubborn. Closed.

"Where is she?" she begs. "Why have they all gone?"

"What is that to you?"

"I have to know," Rita says desperately.

"These things are none of your concern. Let sleeping dogs lie."

"What dogs?" yells Rita. "Where do they lie? Who is Pearce's father?" she screams at the closing door.

The woman's white fists are tight.

"You go away!" she shouts. "I will not be grist for your mill anymore!"

Cannot run, you cannot hide. *The dead dance on.* All the time, there they dance.

Rita shuffles down the path through the autumn leaves as crisp and dry as despair.

"Who is Pearce's father?" she asks Sage.

"Pearce doesn't have any father. She was born to a girl."

"There had to be some man. You can't just spring from nothing. Not even her."

"Her mother was a kid, I think. A kid with a baby. It's dumb, it doesn't work. What would you do with something like that?"

"What did *she* do?"

"Left," says Sage. "Up and left. What's it to you?"

"I'm curious. There's this great, fat, sloppy mystery."

"Nobody knows. Not even Pearce."

"Pearce doesn't give a shit," Rita says scornfully.

"Why do you?"

"I don't know. I just do."

10

Lorraine is brushing out her waist-length, copper-coloured hair after her weekly shampoo, and Sage is watching.

"It makes you look like Lady Godiva," says Sage. She combs through it with her fingers, raking down the full length. "Why do you always put it back up?"

Her mother begins to separate the hair into plaits.

"I really ought to have it cut. I'm too old for all this hair," she says.

"If you do, give some to me to save."

Lorraine laughs. "Whatever would you do with a box of hair?"

"Voodoo, maybe. I could cast spells and hexes. Or I could make a wig out of it."

"Witches get burned," says Lorraine. "But a wig would be interesting."

"I won't ever have long hair."

Lorraine starts braiding. "Your father loved this hair."

"Did you like having sex with Daddy?" Sage asks.

"He spoiled me for anyone else."

"Don't you want another boyfriend?"

Her mother sighs. "It's so hard. I wonder sometimes if I'm wasting my life. And I know he's not coming back."

"And *I* wonder about sex," Sage says.

"What is it you wonder?"

"How do you know when it's right?"

Lorraine sweeps the bottom part of hair over her shoulder to finish the braid. "I wonder about that too."

"Most of the kids I know are either doing it, or thinking about doing it."

"What about you?"

"Just fooling around," says Sage quickly. "Nothing serious."

"Well," Lorraine says. "If it gets serious, you have to use protection."

"I know all about that. I will."

"I don't want you to get pregnant."

"I know."

"Boys don't often think about it."

"I think they do," says Sage.

The braid is done. "Thanks for helping me," says Lorraine.

Sage laughs. "I didn't do anything."

Nelson works the gas pumps at the Petro on the highway. He drops by the theatre after he gets off shift in the evening to watch Sage clean the popcorn machine.

"I got beer in Dad's truck," he tells her. "Let's you an' me go cruising."

"I don't know," says Sage. "What do you really want?"

"I wanna get laid."

Sage looks him over, head-to-feet.

"What's in it for me?"

"Pleasure," he says. "Believe it."

"I think Rita's waiting."

"What d'ya need *her* for?"

"I don't know . . . okay, I'll go."

Rita arrives at the theatre in time to see Sage climbing into Nelson's dad's truck. She presses on her horn, but Sage doesn't notice.

Parks in her usual spot in front of the lobby window. A car full of kids drives by; someone moons her through the rear window.

Rita rests her chin on the steering wheel.

Nelson starts meeting Sage every night after he shuts down the gas pumps.

Rita, hanging over Sage's candy counter, looks him over with narrow cat eyes. At his cool leather jacket to go with his tough-guy Yamaha.

"Let's go, babe! I got the bike," he says.

"Pretty soon it's going to snow," says Rita. "You'll have to start walking again."

"I got my eye on a beater. Reclining seats."

"Where are you going?"

"There's a party at Ralph's," says Nelson.

"You don't have to freeze on his bike all night. I'll give you a ride home," Rita offers.

Sage prods blackened kernels through the metal slots at the bottom of the popper. "It's still early. I think I'll go with Nelson."

"Then I guess I'll see you," says Rita.

"Why's she always hanging around?" asks Nelson. "Tell her to get a life, for crissakes."

"Shut the fuck up," snaps Sage. "Quit trying to think and we'll get along just fine, okay?"

At least on the bike, she doesn't have to listen to him talk.

At Ralph's later, Sage smokes, gets high and hot.

Underneath his clothing, Nelson is stiff. She tugs him down on top, urges him inside. Deep. Deeper. She presses him into herself and locks him there, hard.

Nelson pushes to his own rhythm, not hers.

"Slow down," she says. "Stay there for a minute."

Wants to feel. Wishes Rita's tongue was on her now.

But he just keeps on moving, possessed by his own need.

She's left wanting more. Wanting Rita.

Still hot and wanting Rita.

Eddie is breathless, out of breath from trying to catch up to Rita. "Hey Rags!" he calls. "Wait up!"

She slows down, waits.

"I wanted to walk with you," he pants. "But you left the office so fast, you didn't hear me."

"I'm sick and tired of this place, Eddie. One more school board or parent complaint about our paper and I'm going to give it up. They can't control what we *think*, can they?"

"They sure can try."

"I've had it! I'm so sick of those old farts telling me what I can and cannot print, what this school will *tolerate*, which is *nothing*, I can't stand it!"

"You want to go for coffee with me?"

Coffee at the Chinese Cafe on Main Street is gritty and thick, but fifty cents a cup with endless refills.

"You're the best editor the *Gazette*'s ever had. You don't let them push us around," Eddie says.

"Then why do I always feel so helpless? When that old Peters starts on me, I feel like I'm ten years old, like he's my father. That condom story needs to be published."

"I think old Peters is scared. Scared the school board's gonna shut us down. Scared he's gonna get in shit."

"If we tell them about condoms, everyone's going to rush right out and screw? Half the kids in school are doing it anyway. And it's not cool to use them."

"Guys think it means they're gay."

"I'm printing that fucking story."

"I know." Eddie grins. "That's because you're the best goddamn editor the *Gazette*'s ever had."

Rita cools down when she talks. She always does. Talks herself around the circle and back home. All Eddie has to do is listen.

He leaves her at her doorstep.

Walks back to his father's house under a grey, drizzling sky, thinking about Rita. *I'm in love,* he tells himself. *In love with Rita who's in love with Sage. I haven't got a chance.*

Pearce is pregnant. But she won't allow any *baby* to ruin her life.

She returns to the clinic where she got her birth control prescription to take care of it.

"Those pills you gave me didn't work," she says. "Just tell me what I have to say to get it done and I'll say it."

The counsellor refers her to a psychiatrist.

"He'll authorize an abortion if he's convinced continuing this pregnancy will endanger your physical or mental health," she says.

Pearce snorts. "Does completely fucking up the rest of my life count?"

The shrink calls her *hostile* and recommends an abortion.

Then she waits and waits for them to call her to the hospital while that thing inside gains strength from her.

She talks to Bill at work. It is his responsibility now, this state of her womb. He offers to pay for an abortion across the border.

Bill hasn't figured out his life yet. He has *this wife* and *these two cute kids,* and he's a top-selling salesman of car parts. But he says he's *not happy*. He says he's *attracted to men*. He whispers that he thinks maybe he's *gay*. Cries about his confusion and Pearce urges him to break away.

But, he says, he has *that innocent wife and those two adorable kids who need him. The company needs him. What would happen to all those people who need him* if he *just fucks off to follow his prick?*

Bill is a serious Catholic. He can't approve of abortion, but neither can he approve of sex outside of marriage. With anyone who's not his wife.

He can't go with her, but he gives her money and off she goes. To a clinic across the border where there are no waiting lists and no referrals.

In two hours she is back on the Greyhound. Going home to Canada stoned on painkillers.

"It's all done," she tells him on the phone.

He sends her two dozen florist roses.

Get well soon, says his card.

Okay, she thinks. *You too.*

Patsy always comes to visit Fridays, brings wine, and cooks while Pearce works on her writing. Then they eat and fuck, and sometimes they go out.

Quilted jackets, peasant skirts, bleached-out hair. Bold with lust.

"Are you ready to eat?" she asks.

"Just one more sentence."

"Can I read it so far?"

"Not yet," Pearce says, closing the typewriter. "It smells great. You're such a good cook, Patsy."

"I guess I have to tell you," says Patsy over dessert. Then she sighs.

"What?"

"I'm getting married."

"Married? Why?"

"My mom says, and my dad says, and Joe says, and I have to do it. They all say it's time."

Pearce pushes away her dessert.

"I thought we were friends," she says.

"I can't see you anymore. Besides, you don't want a friend, you never have. You don't need a friend, you need a *toy.* A toy can be anyone, it doesn't matter if it's me. Joe, he cares that it's me."

"I'll miss you Patsy," Pearce says, and this is truth. "I will miss you like anything."

11

"After grad, we'll share an apartment in the city," Rita says.

"I think we should make other plans," says Sage.

Rita is quiet.

"Now what?"

"Do you want to live with Nelson?"

"We've talked about it," admits Sage.

"Is he even going to graduate?"

"He's not totally dumb."

"I didn't even know he was planning to leave town."

"He wasn't."

"I thought he'd work at the Petro till he dies."

"Cut the shit, Rags."

"I don't think you should live with him."

"You're jealous," says Sage. "Face it."

"Why should I pretend to be happy to share you? Nelson's a creep."

"Is not. He makes me laugh. Unlike you, always so deadly serious."

"Not always. Just with you, because I love you so much."

"Jealous," Sage repeats scornfully. "Of Pearce, who isn't even around. Of Nelson. You're sick."

"I don't like sharing. It's not in me."

"With all those fucking brothers, you should at least be used to it. One, two, three," Sage counts on her fingers in Rita's face. "Three brothers! You act like an only child, some queen."

"I don't have anything of my own and it's because of all those stupid brothers. My mother says my needs should come last."

"Your mother's a slave to your fucking family."

"And Lorraine isn't? My family is not my fault," says Rita, sternly. "I didn't choose to be born there."

"I know," Sage says quickly. "But you have to try to control that jealousy of yours. At least with me."

"*You* are my only jealousy."

"If anyone should be jealous, it should be me. You're with Eddie all the time these days."

"We're working on the *Gazette*," Rita says. "All this work has to be done before grad."

"I'm just saying . . . "

"Are you jealous?"

"Of *Eddie*? Of course not." sniffs Sage.

"That's because you know I love *you*."

"I also know you don't go for guys."

"But Nelson . . . " says Rita. "He's not very bright, you have to admit. At least Eddie has brain."

"I like the sex," snaps Sage. "He doesn't need any brain."

Rita invites Sage to the *Gazette*'s year-end party at Lee's parents' house, but Sage says she's busy. Then Eddie calls.

"What kind of booze do you want?" he asks.

"Something sweet," says Rita.

"Dad says I can use his car. I'll pick you up, if you want."

He brings syrupy apricot brandy and reefer, and they smoke in the Oldsmobile on Lee's driveway. Then Eddie opens the car windows to air it out.

Rita drinks her apricot brandy straight from the bottle. Sweet and thick like toffee on her tongue, and searing hot down her throat. *Gazette* staffers give her presents. An engraved plaque, fresh-cut flowers, and a mug embossed with her name.

Eddie hovers, sparkling stars in his eyes.

Their party ends at dawn.

"Fuck!" Rita laughs. "I've never been this high."

Eddie pulls the Oldsmobile over onto a deserted country churchyard, by the gravestones.

Rita giggles at his fingers teasing at her mouth, wriggles when he touches breathlessly at the bare skin underneath her skirt. Slides forward in her seat, spreads her legs.

"Can I do this?"

Rita nods, eyes squeezed shut. "Lick me there," she says sleepily.

"Like this?"

She imagines it is Sage's tongue, caresses his hair with her eyes shut tight. "Sage," she calls when she starts to come.

Eddie tugs at himself, releases on his dad's Oldsmobile seat, between her knees. "I love you, Rita," he cries, voice breaking.

"It's okay, Eddie," Rita croons, opening her eyes.

He rests his head against her shoulder and she soothes him there, in the deep night.

After that night, Eddie makes a wide space between himself and Rita.

"What the fuck did you do to Eddie?" asks Sage.

"Nothing, why?" Rita retorts.

"He's acting strange," says Sage. "It looks like he's avoiding you."

"He asked to take me to grad and I said no. Now he's sulking."

"You're lying."

"In other words," Rita snaps, "mind your own business."

Friday nights aren't the same without Patsy. Bill leaves his wife and kids, and calls Pearce when he gets scared. There are dragons lurking everywhere.

She stops writing Manma, then bathes herself in guilt. Saves up money to cover what she borrowed from that tin and wires a money order. There's no response but it isn't sent back either.

Manma never was a talker. Never talked about anything at all. She paid all her debts, she said. Duty to bone and flesh.

Time blurs.

Crawling out of some stranger's bed, teeth gritty like sucking gravel.

Picks up a shirt from scattered clothing littered on the floor.

Beer bottles line the wall down a narrow white hallway, a crumb trail to the bathroom at its end. Braces against the toilet, pulls herself upright.

This man's bathroom is done in chocolate brown. Tentacles trickle from a Boston Fern suspended above the bathtub. Crunchy dead brown droppings line the bathtub floor.

Eases into the tub, feet wrapping around those dead leaves crisp and hard between her toes. Ducks her head under the shower faucet and rinses.

Shoves damp arms into shirt sleeves, sees her strange face in the mirror above the sink.

Back home, Pearce sucks milk from the carton and then pukes and pukes until she is clean again. Until she recognizes her face in the mirror. Until all traces of his tongue have been erased from her mouth.

Tries to call Patsy but Joe answers the phone so she hangs up without saying anything.

How do you find a dead woman? Dragon-slayers don't exist.

Pearce reads tombstone names.

Katie, Katherine, Catherine, Cathy, Katja, Kay.

There are a lot of dead Ks on the coast, a lot of graveyards.

All she had has been lost. Mementos: some marred photographs and useless, ancient, little-girl schoolbooks. The rest is empty space.

Searching for Katie takes up a lot of time.

KTL paints.

Houses, bathrooms, fences, pictures. Pictures when she can. Stays real with a paintbrush in her hand.

For a moment once she had a real life, then she was a painter.

But Real World came and went. She scarcely knows it now, even when it taps her on the forehead.

***Baby pretty pretty baby** paint Daddy a picture,* says the man with the wide white smile.

12

"You bore me. Really Nelson, you just bore me silly."

Nelson stops wiggling the carburetor linkage and looks up. "Are you on the rag?"

"Yeah, right," says Sage. "You're the most boring guy in this town, maybe even in the whole country. I'm sitting here hour after hour, watching you fiddle with this fucking truck, and I can't believe it. Why am I doing this? For what?"

Nelson wipes his fingers, one at a time, as though he's just finished a meal of fried chicken. "So what you're saying is you wanna be doing something else."

"I'd rather be in math class. I'd rather be at the dentist. I'd rather be drowning in the gravel pit. You bore me to death."

"Because I'm working on the truck?"

"I'm talking about more than just the truck."

"You want me to do something else?"

"I just don't want to go out with you anymore."

Nelson lifts a wrench, and stares at her. His jaw muscles clench. "I get it," he says finally. "They're right about you after all."

"Who's right about what?"

"Everybody. I'm too much man for you."

"Oh shit! I just don't want you. Plain and simple."

"So you and fag Rita are gonna go to grad together," says Nelson hoarsely, "and I'm gonna look like an idiot."

Sage gets up from the grass where she's been sitting cross-legged, watching him toy with the truck. "You don't need any help for that."

"This is your last chance. If you leave now, don't you ever come crawling back. You and me are through."

"C'est la fucking vie," Sage says over her shoulder.

"Fuck you, cunt!" yells Nelson.

Sage shrugs off his curse. "Have a nice life," she yells back.

"Nelson's taking Irene to grad," Rita reports later.

"Good for them," says Sage. "Those two deserve each other."

"I dumped Nelson," says Sage, sinking her teeth into Lorraine's hot rye bread. "This is yummy bread."

Lorraine holds the dripping ladle over Sage's bowl. "Have more soup."

Sage nods and her mother refills her bowl.

"I didn't like him," Lorraine says.

Sage swallows, scoops up more soup. "Rita hates him too."

"I don't know about *hate*. I think you're too smart for him. I don't want you to spend your life as a mechanic's wife."

"All I want is a nice guy like Daddy. Except who'll stick around."

"He phoned last night."

Sage scrapes at the bottom of the bowl. "Where is he now?"

"On the west coast, working, he said."

"So he didn't want money?"

Lorraine sighs. "He's got a lot of debts."

"Maybe he should stop playing the horses."

"He's got an addiction. He needs help."

"Tough love, Mom. Stop bailing him out."

"How did Nelson take it?"

"He's a jerk: he acted like a jerk. He tried to tell me he's *too much man* for me."

"Maybe you're *too much woman* for him," Lorraine laughs. "I told your father about your grad. He said he'd like to be here."

"Right." Sage gathers her bowl and cutlery to carry to the sink. "But he won't be."

"I offered to send him airfare," says Lorraine. "He said he wouldn't be able to make it."

"What else is new. I'll do these dishes later. I've got to get to the theatre now."

"Never mind about them. Have a good night."

Sage pecks at her mom's cheek.

Lorraine gets up slowly to clear the table. *She'll be gone soon, and then what?*

"Who's taking you to grad?" Rita's mother asks.

"I'm going by myself."

Her mother is swallowing Valium by the truckload and Rita spends half her time dying to shake the shit out of her, the other half feeling guilty.

"Yourself," Mother repeats.

"Yeah."

"Who'll buy your corsage then?" she asks, flipping through file cards in her memory bank.

"Shit," Rita says. "I don't need a stinking corsage. If I do, I can buy my own. Or you and Dad can buy me one."

"What about a dress?"

"What *about* a dress?"

"What will you wear?"

"Long johns!" Rita says impatiently and her mother blinks. "It's alright, Mom," she says quickly, now that guilt is rusting up her tongue. "We're renting tuxedos."

Her mother looks confused. "Tuxedos?"

Rita looks at the floor, wishing it could swallow her right now.

"It's sort of a joke," she explains. "Because we're not going with dates."

"Your brother wore a tuxedo."

"I know."

"I never actually believed he'd graduate. I thought he'd be like his father. Never finished high school. It just wasn't in him."

"At least Dad had the store. From his father."

"Of course, I was pregnant by then and he had to work. We had to get married."

"Oh," Rita says. "So you didn't graduate either."

"What for? I was pregnant."

"Well, I'm not," says Rita. "Pregnant."

"Good girl!" Her mother shuts her eyes.

Rita is let go.

She visits the shoe store.

Miriam is there. "Your dad's gone out for lunch," she tells Rita.

"I need a pair of boots," Rita says.

"We have new stock. Look around."

Rita brushes her fingertip across a shiny black boot toe on the shelf in front of her. "When's he coming back?"

Miriam checks the clock behind the counter. "Any minute now. Just look at these, aren't they gorgeous?"

The bell over the door tinkles.

"Speak of the devil," says Miriam brightly.

"Are you here to see me, or are you looking at shoes?" her dad asks.

"Boots. For grad. Miriam's getting them for me."

Rita's dad stands awkwardly. His blond eyelashes make his face seem naked. His huge square shoulders are pushed too snugly inside his suit jacket. But at least he has no beer belly, not like most of the old guys in town.

He never seems to know what to do with his hands. His eyes flirt with the shelves, with the windows.

"Miriam!" he calls. "Are you finding the boots?"

"They're for graduation Daddy," Rita says. "I'll also need some money for clothes."

Now his hands have a job. He reaches into a pocket, takes out his chequebook.

"How much?"

"About a hundred. There's a party afterwards too."

He writes the cheque, snaps it, hands it to Rita, looks away while she tucks it inside her shirt pocket.

"I'll be moving out after grad," she says. "Maybe I'll live with Sage. We don't know yet. But I'll be leaving right away."

"To do what?"

"I've got a job with Bell for the summer. And then I start university in September."

Miriam emerges with three boxes.

"Good for you!" he says heartily. "I knew you had it in you. Miriam," he says, "My Rita's going to university!"

"You must be so proud," she says.

"You betcha."

"Dad, could I get a pair of these for Sage too?"

"Just write it up," he says. "No problem."

"Irene's telling everyone at school that I'm queer," says Sage.

"Who said?"

"Everyone." She rubs her hand across her forehead, feeling where the wrinkles will be when she's older.

"What are you telling them?"

"It'll just get worse if I deny it. I've been saying Nelson turned me off guys."

Rita giggles.

"Soon we'll be out of here."

Sage, completely naked except for those gleaming boots.

"Do you like the boots?"

"They're great! I especially like it that your dad gave them to me."

"He's got this guilt-thing. He had no choice."

"Is he guilty about that woman he's got on the side?"

Rita shrugs. "You name it, he's guilty."

"Irene and Nelson are screwing all over town. Everyone's seen them somewhere, going at it. You'd think they'd never done it before or something. Like it's a completely new invention."

"At least they're not *queer*."

Rita tweaks Sage's bare nipples, one-at-a-time.

Sage grabs her wrists. "Stop that, you!"

"Make me!"

"Okay, I will."

Wrestles Rita flat down on the attic mattress until Rita pleads *stop*.

13

Rita makes her valedictory speech wearing a tuxedo and her tassel. She talks about *the value of freedom*.

No one here knows what the fuck I'm talking about, she thinks, smiling at polite applause.

Her mother's home with a sick Timmy and her dad's at the shoe store. But Lorraine's there, beaming.

The ceremony's in the afternoon; party at night. In between, Rita's parents take her and Sage out to dinner. Rita convinced Sage to come.

"Ask Lorraine too," she said.

"She won't," said Sage but she asked anyway. "She said she'd be out of place."

So it's just the four of them, out for dinner. Rita's dad has pre-ordered their meal and it's all ready for them. He's even ordered wine.

Rita giggles when the waiter pours hers first and waits for her to taste it. She wrinkles her nose, says it's *fine,* and he fills the other glasses.

Her mother drinks quickly, then stares at nothing until her salad arrives.

Her dad makes small talk at first, and then Sage starts talking and the room fills with their laughter. Rita watches and listens, but she doesn't have anything to add.

Her dad looks different. Younger. Almost handsome, even to Rita.

Her mother floats away from time to time, but only Rita notices.

"Are you going to share Rita's apartment?" her dad asks Sage.

"Depends."

"On what?"

"On if you pay our rent," says Sage demurely.

Rita stomps the heel of her boot as hard as she can on her toe. Sage just grins.

"I'm paying whatever she wants," he says, tilting the wine bottle to his glass. "She's my only daughter, after all. What's it all for, anyway, if I can't help out my little girl?"

He twists his finger in the air and the waiter brings another bottle. Refills Sage's glass with a gesture from Rita's father.

Sage drinks more; her face animated, then tired.

"We've got to go get ready for the party now," Rita says. Mother is nodding over her dessert. "Mom!" she says loudly.

Her mother jerks, once.

"Daddy, help her up," says Rita. Her mother limp as a rag doll, nodding like an idiot. "Daddy!" she hisses.

Her father snaps to attention. Pulls his wife up, drags her through the lobby and out to the car.

"Are you coming with us?" he asks, after he's slammed the door on her mother.

"I've got the Volvo," Rita says. "Thanks for dinner."

"I had fun," says Sage.

"Anytime," he says. "That's what fathers are for."

"Your house is always so clean," says Rita.

"Don't you start on me," Sage says.

"Hi Lorraine," Rita says. "You should've come with us for dinner."

"Did you two have a good time?"

Sage drapes her arms around her mother's shoulders. "I missed you, Maw."

"Is she drunk?" Lorraine demands.

"Not really," says Rita. "My dad bought wine. Maybe she had a little too much, but she's okay."

"He kept filling up my glass. That was good wine, though. Wasn't that good wine? He's alright for an old guy. Too bad he's married."

Rita tucks her hand around Sage's elbow. "Let's get ready for our party now," she coaxes.

"I want pictures before you go," Lorraine calls.

The parking lot is filled. The old school building bright.

"Don't make me go in there," Sage begs, tugging Rita's arm.

"This's the last time we ever have to be with these people," says Rita. "Let's show them."

"Show 'em what?"

"How much better than them we are."

"There's that creep Nelson."

"And here's Eddie. Do you ever look spiffy, Eddie."

"Hi, Rags," says Eddie. "Will you dance with me tonight?"

"First and last."

"You were gonna dance with *me*," grumbles Sage.

"Why did you have to go and get drunk?"

"She's dancing with *me*," Sage tells Eddie.

"Okay, okay," says Eddie quickly.

"First *and* last," Rita repeats.

"Who's gonna dance with *me*?" Sage whines.

"All the guys want to dance with you," says Eddie. "They've just been waiting for you to dump that jerk."

"All those guys are just after one thing," Sage says grimly.

"To dance with *you*," he says.

Rita's head tucked under Eddie's chin, she's close and tight. Her breasts push against his shirt.

"I'm going to miss you, Rags," says Eddie softly.

"I thought you were mad at me."

"Not mad."

"We've had some pretty good times."

"I'm sorry about that night. I shouldn't have . . . taken advantage of you like that."

"You didn't," says Rita. "I didn't even know you thought that."

"You were high."

"I don't think you forced me. I think I wanted it. I think I liked it."

"But you don't even love me. You love Sage."

She misses a step, bumps his knees. "Jesus Eddie, keep your voice down!"

"Don't worry, no one can hear."

"What makes you say that?"

"I just know."

The music ends and they're still dancing. "Who you love is your own business, not mine. And not anyone else's."

"Dance with Sage too. Please."

"Sure," says Eddie.

Her last dance belongs to Eddie but she dances with Sage too, fast dancing not for couples. Word gets around Sage is drunk and maybe horny, and the guys without dates crawl all over her. Everyone knows she's no virgin, not after Nelson.

Sage falls into Rita at the table with the punch bowl. "Somebody's put booze in it," she says.

"You've had enough," says Rita, grabbing Sage's plastic tumbler.

Sage tugs back and the plastic cracks. "Now look what you did!" she shouts.

"If you don't shut up, we're going to get thrown out."

"These guys are like tomcats," Sage growls.

Then someone taps her shoulder and she stumbles off to dance.

The last dance, and Rita's head rests against Eddie's chest.

"Wanna do something after?"

"I'm going to Sage's for the night."

"Oh," says Eddie.

"There's only her mom. Not like my place, with kids screaming at seven in the morning."

"Let's go outside."

"Now?"

"Yeah."

"We're dancing."

"We can dance outside."

"In the parking lot?"

"Why not?"

"Where's Sage?"

"She's with Deetz," says Eddie.

"Okay then," says Rita.

The air is chilly, the country sky lit up completely with full moon. Eddie waltzes Rita around the shrubbery beside the school where there is only moonlight. The scent of flowers. The caressing ripple of fresh June leaves.

They are quiet, the two of them, breathing.

"It's been a rough year," Eddie says at last.

"I know," Rita agrees.

"But we won some battles."

"I guess."

"You fought for your editorial licence."

"In some ways."

"Next year, it'll be easier for them. And the next year even more. And so on. All because of you."

"Maybe they won't want it," says Rita. "The freedom. When, or if, they get it."

"Maybe. But, if they do, well . . . "

"It doesn't feel like I accomplished much."

"Well, you did," Eddie says. "And mostly on your own."

"You helped."

"I stood behind you."

"Beside," says Rita.

"I wish we could do it again."

"I think the dance is over," says Rita. "I think the music's stopped."

Sage tumbles out, propped up by bookend guys, one on each arm. "Ree-tah! It's time to go-ho!"

"Over here!"

"Sheldon has beer! Come on!"

"Will you come, too?" Rita asks Eddie.

"My car or yours?"

"Mine."

At Sheldon's house, Sage is being courted by Sheldon and Deetz and Murray.

Rita and Eddie find a dark corner where Rita can keep an eye on Sage and still talk. Smoke is being passed.

"Uh-oh," Eddie says. "Remember last time we did this together."

"So? Pass it here."

"Let's go outside."

Sage is hanging over Deetz's shoulder, Murray's hand is between her knees. They're all laughing.

"We're going outside," Rita tells them.

Sage grins. "Be good."

"I really hate her sometimes," Rita says. "Let's sit in my car."

"Look at that moon!"

"I bet I could miss this kind of sky."

"You're lucky to be getting out."

"Scared too."

"I wish I didn't have to stay here. I have to work in my old man's store free for a year before I can go to university."

"I know."

"Even though I got a scholarship. It's a family rule, he says, can't be broken. I have to *earn my right* to go to school."

"It's not fair," Rita says.

"You're going to live with her?"

"If she decides she wants to."

"I think she's out of her mind if she doesn't."

"Would you live with me?"

Then Eddie is kissing her mouth, licking at her eyelashes. And Rita's kissing him back.

There's moon washing through the car, bathing them in milky light.

"Where's Sage?" Rita asks breathlessly between kisses.

"Never mind her," whispers Eddie. "She's inside, with the guys."

His mouth locks around her nipple and Rita sighs.

"Okay," she says. "I'll do it. Just this once. With you."

Deetz is all over her like some dirty shirt.

"Where's Rags?" asks Sage.

"She left with Eddie," says Deetz. "It's you an' me, babe."

"Eddie?" Sage asks.

"They fucked off," says Deetz. "Right, Mur?"

"Yup," says Murray. "Them two fucked off."

Murray is hunched over the coffee table with a baggie, picking out seeds.

"Roll another," Deetz tells him. "She needs a little more."

"Awright!" Murray says.

At some point, Sage says *no*.

But by that time, it's much too late. Too late to make any difference to Deetz and Murray.

To make any difference to Sage.

Much too late.

14

Eddie steps carefully around the beer cans that litter the rec room floor. Gropes for the bathroom light. Winces at the bold fluorescent. Opens his fly to piss. It burns a little but, from what he's read, that's normal the first few times.

He imagines he looks older, but the mirror doesn't tell him so.

Rita, Rita, Rita. Brain dances around her name. *Rita.* Wraps his mouth around it. *Rita.* Sings it to himself. Brushes his teeth around her name, rinses his face.

Crawls into his cot in his makeshift bedroom behind the furnace.

Remembers Rita's skin, taut nipples, palmful breasts.

He's hard again.

How wet she was down there. Inside those folds. How her skin stretched around his, how all of him fit. How he wanted to go on forever, clutched together like that with *Rita*.

Eddie's got a fistful now, and how will he sleep, ever again?

Sage awakens to a headful of wild sunlight. The house smells like cinnamon. Cinnamon buns and freshly ground coffee.

Rita never made it back. She and Eddie got lost somewhere.

Maybe they finally did it. Maybe Rita liked it. Maybe she'll want more. Maybe she'll back off for a change.

Sage stretches, gives herself a calf cramp. Spends the next few minutes beating at her leg.

Hobbles down the hallway to the washroom. It hurts when she pees.

Of course, she's got her period. Better late than never. At least she won't have to wonder which one did it. *Deetz* or *Murray*. Or *shit-face Nelson*.

Lorraine's in the kitchen, pulling buns from a hot oven. "Good morning," she says cheerfully. "Just in time for these."

"I don't think I can eat," grumbles Sage. "I got this cramp in my leg. And I got my period."

"Poor baby. Where's Rita?"

"I think she decided to go home after all," says Sage, slumping in her chair. "She took off with Eddie, and I didn't see them again."

"Are Rita and Eddie an item?" Lorraine sets a glass of milk down in front of her daughter.

Sage giggles. "An *item*?"

"You know, do they like each other?"

"Eddie's crazy about Rita. He's been lusting after her since junior high." Sage bites into a sticky bun.

"But not her, huh?"

"She's, well . . . She doesn't really go for guys."

"I think Rita likes you," says Lorraine carefully. "I've always thought so."

"We're best friends. Of course she likes me."

"*Likes* you, I mean. Lusts after you."

Sage swallows too much at once and her mother hits her back until she coughs it up.

"*I* like guys," Sage says, shoving the buns to the centre of the kitchen table. "You should know that. Really, mother!"

"In a small town like this, it's not easy being different. But I don't think it's such a bad thing, I think it's just another way of loving. There's all kinds of strange things people do."

Sage stares at her mother. "Are you saying you're lesbian?"

Lorraine laughs. "I'm nothing. I just said I don't think it's so bad. I've never minded about Rita."

"You sure minded Pearce."

"That was completely different. Entirely."

"Different, how?"

"She was much older than you. It didn't seem balanced, for one thing. And you loved her too much and I don't think she knew how to love you back."

"I don't love Rita."

"I wonder if you could live without her though."

"Sure I could."

Sage grabs another bun and bites hard.

"Did you drink last night?"

"A bit."

"Do you have any cause for regret?"

"I don't remember. Jeez, Mom. If the people in this town knew what you're really like, they'd ride you out on a rail."

"Nobody here really knows me. I wish I had a good friend."

"Did you ever have a best friend?"

"Do you want some coffee now?"

Sage nods. Lorraine pours.

"I had one," she says, "but she left town. And then your dad . . . he was my best friend for a while."

"Who was it who left?"

"She had a lot of problems," Lorraine says.

The phone rings.

Sage leaps up.

"Where did you guys go?" she's asking. "You were supposed to come here after."

Rita couldn't sleep after she left Eddie at his car in the school parking lot.

She spent the rest of her grad night under the sky, watching it change from midnight blue to teal to rust to crimson to gold.

Then she parked the Volvo at her parents' house and crept up the stairs to her own bedroom.

By the time she crawled into her bed, she could hear her father rinsing his teeth and pissing. Soon Timmy would tiptoe into her room. And then she'd have to get up to get him breakfast and settled in for morning television.

Rita thinks about Eddie, how it was with him before and after.

Not so bad, she thinks sleepily. *Not as bad as I thought it'd be.*

Shuts her eyes around her thoughts, squeezes them in tight.

Gentle. Soft all over. Even where he was hard, where he was supposed to be hard, his skin around was soft.

He licked at her like some eager puppy.

When he pushed himself inside, it didn't even hurt. She became wet, wet and pliant and elastic. Stretched around him like some glove.

Stop it, thinks Rita, *this isn't me. This is something else.*

I've never wanted any guy before.

Rita sleeps after all.

15

Timmy helps her pack the Volvo. She calls Sage when it's done.

"I'm all packed. Are you coming?"

"Yeah," says Sage. "Where did you guys go? You were supposed to come here after."

"You were taken care of. So Eddie and me took off."

"Lorraine made cinnamon buns for our breakfast."

"Are there any left?"

"Nah, I ate 'em all. Of course there's some left."

"Pack them to eat on the drive."

"What did you and Eddie do?"

"What did you and those guys do?" counters Rita.

"Fuck," says Sage.

"Us too," says Rita. "I'm all packed. I'll be over in fifteen minutes."

"I don't want you to go," Timmy tells her. "Please don't."

"I have to."

"Why do you have to?"

"It's time. I just have to. When you're older, you'll see."

"Will you miss me?"

"More than anything."

His face crinkles and Rita holds him close.

"You'll be okay," she promises.

Her mother comes out to wave goodbye.

Her dad is at the store. Raymond's at work and Danny's out. Just Timmy and Mom.

Rita pulls away from them, waving.

Lorraine is waiting at the door.

"All packed?" she asks, wiping her hands on her apron. "We saved you breakfast."

"Is she ready yet?"

"She only decided to go with you at the last minute. Now she's trying to decide what to take and what to leave."

"Typical. Should I go help her figure it out?"

"Come and talk to me instead," says Lorraine.

At last Sage clatters down the stairs, dragging an old backpack and a battered suitcase.

"Let's get the fuck out of this town," she yells.

"I hate city driving," complains Rita. "I can't see. We shouldn't have packed that stuff so high."

Sage shoves her head through her rolled-down window.

"What do you need to see?"

"Just tell me if you think something really bad's going to happen."

"Like what?"

"Like a major crash or something."

"Hit the brakes!" screams Sage, and Rita slams down.

"What?"

"Yellow light. I thought you didn't see it."

"Do me a favour. Shut the fuck up."

"Check out the guys in the truck. Hey, you!"

"Jesus!" says Rita, her back straight. "Thank goodness we're almost there. Can you read that street sign?"

"I think it's Highland."

Rita stops the Volvo in front of a three-storey red brick house flanked by oak trees.

"We've got the whole second floor," she says.

Sage shoves up the narrow stairs behind Rita.

"I'm sore from all that sitting. Hey, look at those windows!"

"Stained glass. Inside, too. Wait till you see!"

"You should carry me over the threshold."

"You weigh a ton. *You* should carry *me*."

Gleaming old hardwood floors and stained glass. One bedroom. Clawfoot tub. A sunroom. And a narrow kitchen with turquoise cupboards, a pantry with rows and rows of shelves, and a fire escape door.

Sage dashes through.

"Now you've seen it, help me get our stuff in."

"Man, this is great. I love it!"

"You better get a job soon," says Rita. "We have to pay the rent."

"No problem," says Sage.

They unload the car and then wander their new neighbourhood, finding the shops for milk and newspapers.

"We need a television."

"Why?"

"I can't sleep if I don't watch the news."

"I'll get you to sleep."

"It's not the same."

"I'll read to you."

"I need a fucking television," Sage grumbles.

"Get a job and buy one," says Rita.

"You buy it. Get your dad to buy it."

"I don't want one. It eats up brain cells. I'll read to you instead."

"If you wanna be a fucking journalist, you need a television."

"I'm a writer, I won't work for television."

"You've got some lofty morals."

"Let's go to bed and I'll read to you."

"Something dirty, then. *Lady Chatterly's Lover*."

"Is that the dirtiest thing you can think of?"

"What other dirty stuff have you got?"

"I have to unpack my books."

"That'll take forever!"

"No, wait . . . I know exactly where it is. It'll just take a second."

Rita starts to scramble through her boxes.

"I think I'll take a shower," says Sage, sniffing at her underarms.

Rita awakens to early dawn and city traffic sounds and Sage's elbow in her eye.

Takes a second to remember where she is and why. Why she and Sage are in this bed together.

Takes another to consider her blessings.

Then she gets up to brush her teeth. Gets up carefully, without disturbing Sage.

Fumbles with the shower.

Pats baby powder all over, between her breasts and between her legs.

Finds the coffee pot, fills it with water, rummages for coffee.

Wishes she had a newspaper, but she'd have to get dressed to get one.

Wanders down the hall, coffee in hand, past the bedroom where Sage is still snoring, through the front room filled with boxes, to the sunroom.

Perches on the window ledge and peers down through the leaves.

Across the street, a bare-chested fat man pushes a hand-powered mower across his grass. A toddler on a three-wheeler wobbles to and fro along the sidewalk.

Otherwise, the street seems still.

Rita sits naked in her new sunroom drinking coffee.

No one knows who I am, and no one gives a shit. If I sleep with Sage. If I'm naked. No one can see.

After she's done her coffee, she starts unpacking. Books in the built-in shelving, magazines in the rack she took from home. Katherine Hepburn and Bette Davis on the walls. James Dean in the bathroom for Sage. Marilyn Monroe in the kitchen.

Sage crawls out of bed around noon. Comes yawning to the kitchen where Rita has unpacked her meagre supplies.

"Man. Fuck. Coffee," says Sage, filling the mug Rita set beside the pot for her. "Where's the fucking sugar?"

"In the canister. Good fucking morning to you, too."

"Don't be my fuckin' mother."

"I don't want to be your fucking mother," Rita snaps.

"My mother doesn't fuck." Sage slumps at the table, hands wrapped around her coffee mug. "What are we doing today?"

"I'm not your fucking mother," says Rita.

"Gimme a break," Sage whines. "It's way too early."

"You didn't even notice all the stuff I already did."

Sage glances around. "Lovely," she says at last.

"You haven't even seen it all. Like Marilyn?"

"I love fucking Marilyn. In the kitchen, barefoot, where she belongs."

"She's wearing those heels. And you can't fuck her in the kitchen — she's dead."

Rita is in training to be a telephone operator. Mag, with bleached-yellow hair and peacock eyeliner, is teaching her.

"Some of those women have been there for twenty years!" she tells Sage.

Rita learns so quickly she's put on the board in three days.

"The record before was five days. Imagine, five days to learn how to answer a phone!"

Sage sleeps till noon every day. Disappears, then doesn't come home until after midnight.

Rita works shifts, and sometimes sleeps late. When she wakes up, Sage is gone. When she gets home, Sage is gone.

"Leave me a note," Rita tells her.

"I thought you weren't going to be my mother."

"I don't know where you are, or when you'll be back. What if something happens to you? How will I know?

"Nothing's gonna happen to me. I'd phone."

"Are you trying to find a job?"

"You have to get to know people. That's how you find work."

"You find work by looking for a job."

"I'm *looking*."

"In the bar?"

"I'll get a fucking job if that'll make you happy. *Man!*"

"I don't want to have to ask my dad for money all the time. And I especially don't want to have to ask because *you* don't have a job."

"I get your fucking point," says Sage.

In bed, Sage turns away from Rita.

"I don't want to," she says.

"We're living together, we're in the same bed, and now you don't want to. What the hell is wrong?"

"I don't know," says Sage, pushing Rita's hand away. "I just don't want you to touch me."

"All the time, or just right now?"

"What's the difference?"

"Well, if it's all the time . . . "

"Then what?"

"Then I think I don't want to live with you," Rita finishes, rolling on her side and away from Sage.

Her words hang heavy in the bedroom with the crimson wallpaper.

"Rita . . . "

"What?"

"Don't be mad."

"I'm not," says Rita. "I'm just trying to figure this out."

"You can touch me if you want to," Sage says, her voice small.

Rita inhales crimson. Then she rolls over and presses her chin against Sage's hair.

"Not if you don't want me to," she says hoarsely.

Sage sets Rita's hand on her breast.

"I do."

***The girls* at Bell** have a bowling team. They ask Rita to join.

"We just sit around here all the time. It's kinda' nice to do something physical, you know?" Mag says.

"You're fucking *bowling*?" Sage snorts. "Old people go bowling."

"It's something to do. And they asked me."

Sage takes her to the bar where she hangs out now, introduces her to guys: *Jerry. Michael. Stan. Joey. Frank.*

"Are you screwing all of them?"

"No."

"Which ones then?"

"Just Joey."

"Why just him?" asks Rita. "When you could have them all?"

She returns at seven in the morning, exhausted from an all-night shift.

Brushes her teeth.

Strips off her work clothes.

Stumbles down the hallway.

And there's Sage's startled face hanging over some guy's shoulder.

The two of them, in Rita's bed.

Rita growls.

"I forgot," says her white-lipped lover. "Please, Rita . . . I got drunk! I forgot."

"In *my* bed!" Rita screams. "Get him out!"

Rita hasn't slept yet. Eyes filled with dust.

Lifts her mug to drink, her hand shakes.

The sun's been up for hours and Rita's been awake.

Sage got Joey up and dressed and out, and she's been hiding in the bathroom ever since.

It's just a matter of time, Rita thinks. *She'll have to come out eventually.*

But finally she's had enough.

"Come *out,*" she says to the bathroom door.

"I can't," Sage mumbles.

"Are you sick?"

"Scared."

"Of what?" asks Rita coldly.

"You."

"What do you think I'll do?"

There's no answer.

"Come out," Rita says again. "I can't stay awake forever. I have to pee. And you're in trouble, any way you look at it."

Sage opens the door, grinning sheepishly.

"You can pee."

"First I want to talk."

"In the kitchen?"

"There's coffee there."

Sage hangs her head over her coffee cup.

"Okay, give me shit," she says.

"I can't stand this," says Rita grimly. "I don't know why you're doing this, but . . . " Sage is crying now. "Oh, don't cry. I'm pissed off. Please don't cry now."

"I can't help it. I hate it when you're mad at me."

"Why are you doing this?"

"I got drunk and I just forgot."

"You've been screwing around since we got here. Today is just a part of it. And you're not even *trying* to get a job."

"I'm scared."

"Of what?"

"Everything. School. New people. This city."

Rita sighs loudly. "There's two things," she says. "First, find a job. Second, get your own place."

"Please don't make me."

Rita slams her mug into the rust-stained sink.

"I'm going to *my* bed now, to get some sleep before I have to go back to work. You can stay in the living room. And I'm not taking any more shit from you."

Then Sage disappears for two days and nights and Rita is frantic.

She visits the bar.

"Haven't seen her," says Michael. "Coupla days, anyway."

"What about Joey?"

"Him either."

Asks for Joey's phone number, address, but he can't say.

She calls in sick. *Sick with fear, sick with worry.*

"I have the stomach flu, I think," she tells Mag.

Mag tells her to take care of herself.

"Could be food poisoning," she says cheerfully.

It's the third night when Rita's taking a hot bath that Sage comes back.

"Sweetie!" she squeals, arms outstretched.

Relief makes Rita giddy.

"I thought you were dead," she giggles.

"Like my new hair?"

Sage: laughing, twirling. Close-cropped, sultry, new fiery auburn highlights.

"It's beautiful!"

"I got myself a job. Just a crummy waitress job, but what the hell, it's money. It'll help out."

Rita gets busy wrapping herself in her favourite green towel.

"Where's the job?"

"Sobees downtown. Great pizza. You'll have to come, maybe with your *girls* from work."

"Let's celebrate."

"I brought wine. And you can read me something."

They take wine to bed and Rita reads. Sage strokes her. Absently at first.

"It's been a while," she says, drawing Rita's nipple taut between her thumb and forefinger.

"Forever since *you've* touched me," says Rita.

The book drops from her hand to the floor; she lies back.

Sage holds her small, hard breasts under both palms. Rubbing, tugging, kneading.

Rita spreads her legs wide; she touches her clit with the tip of her middle finger, pressing down hard where it feels best. She's throbbing, rubbing herself tight.

"I'm getting wet inside. Feel."

"Say *pretty please*."

"*Pretty please*," Rita says hoarsely.

Sage's hand crawls down Rita's belly, tugs gently at her silky pelvic fur.

Rita squirms, caresses herself while Sage watches.

Massages the hill of her pubic bone. Slides her palm slowly down, skimming over Rita's hand where she is touching herself.

One finger, two, three. In, out, in.

Stirs around inside, fishing for the clenching muscles that mean Rita is coming. Stir, thrust, stir.

"My fingers are drenched," she whispers. "You're so wet."

"Christ!" groans Rita, straining.

First, her sharp release like firewater.

Then the tears.

Sage tastes them hot on Rita's cheek.

16

Their honeymoon is over.

Sage starts her new job and Rita never sees her unless she happens to be off-shift when Sage picks up clothes. Her half of the closet is almost bare; her dresser drawers are emptying.

Rita meets a woman at work. They take coffee break together when they're on the same shift. Loni is older. She's been around.

Loni asks her to go for a drink after an evening shift and Rita says, "Yeah, sure, why not?"

Feeling each other out, cat-and-mouse.

"Do you have a boyfriend?"

"I don't like guys in general."

"Living with someone?"

At closing time, she invites Rita *for a nightcap*.

"Sure," Rita says, "why not?"

Loni has a queen-size waterbed with black satin sheets. An ornate mirror at the foot of her bed.

She undresses for Rita like a stripper. Teases herself. For Rita. Touches herself all over. For Rita's pleasure.

"You like that?" she asks.

Rita nods, horny despite herself.

"I showed you mine, now you show me yours," Loni says.

It's a hot night, a long, hot, steamy night but Rita can't come.

Loni smells odd. Her breasts sag. Her bum is too big. Her voice sounds phony. The mirror by the bed magnifies it all.

Rita's head begins to pound.

"I have to go home," she says at last.

"Did I do something wrong?"

"No, nothing. You're . . . magnificent," says Rita. "It's just . . . I have this headache. Allergies. Nothing personal, nothing to do with you at all."

Sage is in heat. This time with Wayne.

Wayne is the head waiter at Sobees. Hot car, cool clothes.

He flirts with everyone. Customers, men and women, waitresses, the cooking staff.

"Why do you do that?" she asks.

"Do you want me to stop?"

"Nah. I don't care. I kind of like watching."

"Does it turn you on?"

"Sort of," she admits.

"Would it turn you on to watch me fuck someone else?"

"I don't think so," she says, after a minute. Teases at his matted pubic hair with her tongue. "But, maybe . . . with another guy," she says, muffled.

"Hey!" says Wayne, tugging at her hair. "You're some chick, you know that?"

"Right. Some *chick*," she repeats.

Dumps Wayne. Drags all her clothes back to Rita's place.

Rita finds her there after a day shift. Unpacking. "Are you moving in?" she asks.

"Ha, *ha*! He called me a *chick*."

"I don't think you can keep doing this," says Rita. "Moving in and out like this, at the drop of a hat."

"I didn't actually move out."

"You just vanish," snaps Rita. "You don't ever *actually* anything."

Sage drops to her knees, her hands clasped. Crawls over to where Rita is standing sternly by the bedroom door.

"Can I live here please, Miz Rita?" she begs.

Rita starts laughing.

"Oh shit!" she says. "You win. Again."

Sage is spooned around Rita's body, her chin tucked against Rita's shoulder.

"God, I'm so dumb," she mutters.

"You said it," Rita mumbles. "Not I."

"These guys are all such assholes. I don't know why I keep going back."

"It's the only way to be, you keep saying."

"It's different with a guy. I can't explain it."

"It's called a prick, I think."

"You're the only woman."

"What about Pearce?" Rita asks into her pillow.

Sage stiffens. "What *about* Pearce?"

"You were in love with her."

"That was different."

"How?"

"I was a *kid*."

"She's the first one you were in love with."

"So?"

"Your first choice."

"It was adolescent." Sage sniffs. "A crush, a phase."

Rita snorts.

"What?"

"I guess I'm just a continuation of your *phase*."

"You just kept pushing. Like a fucking bitch in heat."

Rita's stomach pulls tight. "You were too weak to resist?"

"Something like that," Sage says angrily. "I was vulnerable."

"You'd better go sleep on the couch."

"Now why are you mad?"

"It's *Pearce* again," yells Rita.

Sage sits up.

"You piss me off, Rags. I haven't seen Pearce since I was thirteen fucking years old! I don't even know whether she's dead or alive. I don't even know *where the fuck she is*!"

Rita jerks up too.

"And all I am to you is *some bitch*! Just a stinking replacement."

"You're still jealous. Of someone who doesn't exist." Sage lays her hands on Rita's bare shoulders. "There's nothing I can do about the past. All I know is that I keep coming back to *you*." Rita's shoulders are trembling. "Please don't cry. I'm so tired of making you cry."

"Do you still love Pearce?"

Sage is silent for a minute.

"Part of me," she says finally. "But that has nothing to do with *us*."

"How can you still love her?"

"I'm just trying to be honest with you."

"After she left you without one word, when you don't even know where she is?"

"I don't know how or why," says Sage. "Believe me, I don't fucking know."

Rita cries in her sleep at night.

Sage, who can't fall asleep in the first place, listens.

What have I done?

Rita's love is searing a hole through her heart.

Sage serves breakfast in bed on a tray. Fresh coffee with real cream, buttered rye bread toast, fluffy scrambled eggs.

"My head hurts," Rita complains. She coughs. "My throat's scratchy. Maybe I'm coming down with something."

Sage plumps the pillow and shoves it back behind Rita's head. "Have some breakfast."

"Where's yours?"

"I already ate."

"How come you're up so early?"

"Just for a change," shrugs Sage. "I watched the sunrise, what I could see of it."

"Are you working today?"

"Day off."

"Oh."

"I thought maybe you'd go to the campus with me."

Rita bites into toast.

"Is that why you're serving me?"

They wander around the university in a daze, embarrassed to ask directions.

"We're hicks," says Sage. "How are we ever going to figure this out?"

"At least we're not dumb hicks."

"This is true."

"Let's find their newspaper office. That's all I need."

They find an old issue in a bin and Rita checks for a room number.

"Let's go there. They can tell us everything we need to know."

17

Today is a good day.

Can see Real World.

Pavement, solid grey matter. People flesh and bone, pink and brown matter. Today she can see through Real World atmosphere, usually thick and dense as ocean fog.

Crisp images, maybe even colour. But colour vision is in the brain not the eyes, and KTL's brain is full and so busy elsewhere.

Big woman, her two or three chins quivering, pounds on a green door. White jelly that is her upper arm wobbles as her fat fist thumps on the green wood. Her skin on the jelly as lumpy as chicken flesh.

KTL's brain says the woman is *disgusting, takes up way too much Real World space.*

Inside her brain, some grotesque baby coos and chortles; drool spittles down its chin. Its two or three chins.

KTL slams the green door on the fat woman's overripe face. Shuts out Real World pictures for now.

Enough is too much, she tells the ugly baby.

After her second abortion, Pearce returns to type invoices.

Larry ogles her ripe nipples brushing against her grey silk blouse with every keystroke. "Let's go for lunch," he says heavily.

Lunch, with her boss Larry at the hotel room, where he nurses the milk from her overfull breasts.

Mrs. Rolstar, Larry's wife, takes an interest in Pearce. Flirts with her all the time. Pearce flirts back.

Mrs. Rolstar makes Pearce her business, takes her to lunches, buys her clothes. Eventually she makes an offer and Pearce doesn't refuse.

Mrs. Rolstar has perfectly manicured breasts underneath expensive clothes; she says she *likes her sex with women rough.*

Pearce makes her call Larry from the bed in the hotel room.

"First you have to call. I'm not losing my job over this."

"Fuck me while I talk," says Mrs. Rolstar.

Pearce sets the phone on her tucked belly.

"Phone," she orders.

"He said *fine,*" Mrs. Rolstar reports, tossing down the phone. "*You girls have fun.*"

"You are an impatient child," says Pearce. "With nasty manners."

She finds the bars where only women go.

Someone in leather takes her home. Strokes her while she weeps.

Mama, Pearce cries.

There, there, the woman croons.

"Hit me," she says. "It's the only way that I can come."

Bad girl. Bad, bare skin, *girl* and, as the stinging starts, *baby, baby, baby* Pearce comes and comes and can't stop.

Throughout, she's still writing, writing, writing.

Pearce dances on air to cash her first-ever cheque from a story.

Thirty-five dollars. Nothing in the grand scheme of things but it's all hers. No one else could have written her story.

Almost anyone could do her job in the parts sales office, anyone who could type, clean, make coffee, and guffaw at *dumb blonde* jokes.

It's just a little mystery story, a few thousand words, but it's all hers.

Calls Patsy.

"Patsy," she says, "I sold a story!"

"Pearce?"

"Did you hear me? I sold a story!"

"I asked you not to phone here again," Patsy says. "It'll just make more trouble."

"There's no one else for me to tell."

18

The city smells like old grass.

Sage is counting down to school on the kitchen wall calendar. "Just fifteen more days," she tells Rita.

"I'm thinking about going home once before school starts," says Rita.

"Lorraine misses me. The house is too empty, she says."

"I haven't talked to my mom for weeks."

"Maybe we should."

"Let's go this weekend."

"I'll call Lorraine."

Sage packs all her dirty laundry into the Volvo. Rita packs clothes for the weekend.

"Maybe I'll even visit the theatre."

"I think I'll call Eddie. Jeez, I hate city driving."

Sage stuffs junk food down her throat all the way: taco chips, chocolate bars, pop.

"How can you eat all that?"

"It helps my stomach."

"Just don't puke. And you better clean up all your crumbs."

"This is too weird, nothing ever changes here. Hey, my street! Hang a right."

"I know where to turn!" snaps Rita.

Lorraine's out, raking.

"I need my stuff," says Sage breathlessly, reaching over the seat.

"At least wait till I've stopped," says Rita, but Sage's door is open and she's flying into Lorraine's outstretched arms.

"Are you coming?" she calls.

"I'm going home," Rita says.

Her parents' house is still as a tomb.

"Mom!" she shouts. "Timmy! Danny!"

Stashes her bag in her old room. Drags the phone from the hallway, sets it between her knees on the bed, and dials Eddie's number.

He answers on the fifth ring.

"Rags!" he screams.

She's sitting on the front steps, smoking, when they get back.

"Hi," she calls. "Can I help you with groceries?"

"In the back," says her mother.

"Come on," Rita tells her brother. "Give me a hand."

Her mother fumbles with the doorknob.

"You look tired, Mom. You want to take a nap?"

"There's too much to do."

"Just sit down then, okay?"

Her mother sits with her feet propped up, watches Rita put the food away.

"Where is everybody?"

"Your father went to the city yesterday. He'll be gone till Monday. Raymond's moved out, you knew that, and Danny's at camp."

"So it's just us?"

Her mother sighs. "Timmy's here. And your dad said he'd call you."

"What's he doing?"

"Buying," says her mother vaguely.

"Winter stock?"

"Seeing his *girl*friend," says Rita's mother.

Rita swallows hard around the words.

"Who's Dad's girlfriend?" Timmy asks.

"Dad's *girl*friend . . . "

"*Mom,*" says Rita quickly. "His girlfriend is Mom, of course! Go put away this toilet paper."

"He's in the city all the time. He's letting Miriam run the store, and Raymond. Spending all his time in the city with that tramp. And I'm here alone."

"Mother," says Rita heavily.

"I'm the laughingstock," says her mother. "Everyone in town knows about your father and his tramp."

"Don't say that," Rita begs.

"It's the truth. Everyone. Hand me that bottle from the fridge."

"Why do you take this stuff?"

"It helps me relax," her mother says, struggling with the safety cap. "Can you open it for me?"

Rita opens the bottle easily and passes it back. Her mother pours blue tablets into her palm and then into her mouth.

"How many of those do you take?"

"I'm going to have a rest," her mother says, getting up heavily.

"Mom . . . "

But there's nothing for her to say. What does she know about it anyway?

Lorraine feeds Sage.

Fresh garden salad. Whole cherry tomatoes, sun-warm and sweet. Hot home-baked bread soaking with butter, and beet borscht with sour cream.

Sage pushes back from the table, unbuttons her shorts.

"I'm stuffed! You're spoiling me, Mom."

"I wish you'd come home more often. It's not so far to drive. Or you could just take the bus sometime."

"I brought my laundry. Rita gave me shit. She said I shouldn't."

"Of course you should! Why pay for a laundromat when I can do it here for free?"

"I'm going out tonight. There's some things I wanna do."

"Oh," says Lorraine. "I thought you'd stay home and we could talk."

"There's still tomorrow."

Eddie stands waiting on the front steps while Rita gets Timmy to bed.

"You could sit at least," she teases. "Unless you have to go right away."

"You look so good."

"You too."

"I'm glad you called."

"Yeah."

Both of them stare out at the street.

"It's so quiet here. I never do this in the city."

"Is it loud where you live?"

"It's a pretty quiet street. For a city. I just never think of sitting outside there."

"How's Sage?"

Rita braids the fringes on her shorts.

"Okay."

"Are you happy?"

"About Sage?"

"Now that she's living with you?"

"It started out that way," Rita says slowly. "But now . . . "

"Now . . . " says Eddie, heart racing.

"It's been a long summer."

"I'm working at the lumber store, selling drywall and paint, and I can't write anymore."

"Nothing?"

"At all. I just lost it. At first, after you left, I wrote like crazy. Like . . . well, love poems to you. Then I dried up. I'm dead here."

"Can I see what you wrote?"

"I'll give them to you, but you can't read them till you get back to the city."

"Mom says my dad is spending all his time in the city. With his girlfriend. She says everyone in town knows."

Eddie says nothing.

"Do they?"

"Well, I've heard gossip."

"Mom's flattened from pills."

"I've heard that, too."

"I cry in my sleep, all the time," Rita says. "And when I wake up, my pillow's wet."

Eddie reaches for her hand, squeezes it.

"What's she doing to you?"

"She's breaking my heart."

"I knew she would. You're way too good for her."

"I love her."

"You should let her go."

Much later, they're lying under the stars in her parents' back yard, holding onto each other. Rita traces the pattern the grass has made on his cheek with her fingertip.

"Sometimes, it feels like we've known each other forever," says Eddie.

"I feel like that sometimes too."

"But we hardly know each other, really," he says absently. "Look at that, a shooting star!"

"I don't even like guys."

"I'm not a guy, I'm an alien from another world."

It's after three when Rita walks Eddie back to his father's house.

"There's lights on," she says. "Does your dad stay up this late?"

"He probably just passed out. He forgets to go to bed."

"Is he still drinking?"

"Yeah." Eddie kicks at the door. "He's never going to stop."

"Does he still beat on you?"

"I'm bigger now. I hit back."

"I'll write."

"Sure you will."

Eddie walks quietly past his snoring father to his own room.

Smiles at the photo of Rita on his bedside table.

Picks up a pen and his small blank reporter's notebook.

Rita lets herself into her parents' house.

A trickle of light seeps out around the frame of her mother's bedroom door.

"Mom?" she calls timidly. There's no answer so Rita goes to bed, waiting out the tears that rock quietly down her cheeks.

She reads Eddie's poems after Sage leaves for work on Sunday night. When she's alone and can hear herself think.

Reads and reads. Then spends a long while looking out through the sunroom windows.

On Monday morning, she tells Sage she's moving out.

"You can either stay here, or find your own place."

"Why now?" Sage asks. "It's been pretty good for us lately."

"That's why."

"I don't get it."

"I don't want to do this when you've brought some asshole into my bed. I want us to stay friends."

"Why do I feel so lousy?"

"You want drama. You want screaming. You want histrionics.

But I've been crying all the time and there's something wrong with that. There's a whole new world opening up for us and we're miserable."

"Speak for yourself," says Sage. "I'm doing great."

"Okay, *I'm* miserable."

"I'm even going down on you. You wanted that and I'm doing it."

"You *hate* doing it. But that's beside the point. I keep waiting for the other shoe to drop. Once you start school, and you meet all those guys, you'll go into heat again."

"I'll be lonely."

"Not for long. Besides, we'll stay friends. But you can't coax me out of this. My mind's made up."

"Don't we have to give notice? I can't afford this place on my own."

"I already did," says Rita. "For the end of August."

Rita gets busy looking for a new place. Her summer job ends, and she spends the last part of August packing and shopping.

Sage plans to keep her waitress job after she starts school.

"I'll need the money. Lorraine has to support Daddy's habits, you know. So I can't count on her."

"Aren't you going to start packing?"

"Why the fuck should I start already? I've got dick-all to pack."

"Have you found a place?"

"Joey got one for me."

"I thought you were finished with him."

"We're still buddies," Sage says. "He's gonna help me move too."

"I get to move into my new place early. So I'll be gone before you. I want my security deposit back."

"How do you get it back?"

"The place has to be cleaned."

"No problem," says Sage. "I'll do that."

Rita moves out on Thursday before the long weekend. Sage is nowhere to be found.

One last slow walk through their apartment, stopping in her sunroom where late morning sun pours through stained glass in prisms of colour. The solid oak outside resisting autumn. That toddler across the street screeches out the words of the *Sesame Street* theme song, and the fat man without a shirt is washing his car.

Rita butts her cigarette firmly on the wide wooden window ledge, and tosses it outside. She'll pick it up when she gets down there, put it in the trash.

This is just another empty apartment now.

Somewhere towards the middle of her brain there stands one girl, motionless. Eyes blink from time to time, but otherwise she stands still.

Around her is greyish billowing cloud.

Grey-matter, KTL's brain tells her. *Girl encased by that grey-matter.*

Outside the real window, one girl stands on the street corner. Eyes vacant, she stares so long at Real World Nothing that it makes her blind.

All that pollution. Thick, Real World atmosphere.

A long silvery car coils like some snake around the corner, hisses, idles. Real World girl snaps to sudden attention, cocks her head, smiles, then climbs into that cold car. A flash of stocking and she's out of sight. The reptile, blazing silver scales, takes her away from her corner.

Look out! shrieks grey-matter-girl in the middle of KTL's brain but it is too late for warning. Real World girl has vanished with the hissing snake.

She will be back, KTL tells her grey-matter-girl, *then look out. The poison from the snake will be lodged inside her, and she will need more to satisfy her demand.*

Not sated? asks grey-matter-girl.

No, KTL tells her, *not sated. Needing more. Every taste of that poison leads to greater need. It is the nature of the beast. Ask me, I know.*

Grey-matter-girl becomes all over sullen, sinks back into captivity. Shuts up where she belongs, inside KTL's busy brain.

19

This has been a long, long path, she tells her grey-matter-girl.

The doctor orders her to *look*, pointing through the passenger side of the windshield, his breath crawling anxious against her skin.

Look! he orders, pointing and she averts her eyes, pretending to obey. *Oh fuck,* he groans. *Aw, look at that.*

Rubs his crotch. Hard, angry head hard. Eyes on that waiting girl at the roadside.

Child really, with heavy mouth and baby fat. Feet urged into heels, as though bound. Bare belly. Princess wants to tell her, *Cover up, you'll die of hypothermia,* but this is the child's bread and butter, who cares?

Child approaches, eager for their warmth and hungry for something else.

Rolls down the window with his spare hand.

How much?

Handjob, fifty, child shivers. *She's extra.*

She's just watching.

Seventy with her.

He gestures, she climbs into back seat. Vinyl on vinyl.

Right at the first corner, left at the next, rubs himself wet.

Child clambers through the seats and wedges between man and woman.

I'll do her for nothin', she offers. *I like girls.*

Scratches on her belly like rivers on a map. Up and down her bare white arms, tracking across her body like a railway line.

No! says Princess.

He introduces child to the flesh he calls his *Leader*, that stem where he carries his anger.

Seventy, she says. *Both.*

Pay the girl, says Doctor.

Princess unravels bills, counts out three twenties and two fives. Wedges them between child's baby flesh and denim exactly as she has been taught.

Child sighs lightly and begins to tug at *Leader* where the swelling starts. Her furtive other hand touches Princess on her thigh, up high, fingernails pressed into weak, weak flesh. Those ripe nails, urgent now with something more than mind can give to word.

They come together. She in stillness; he with angry grunts.

Darkness all around them and fear so pungent, she tastes it deep, layered over her hidden heat.

The dishes can wait, those dishes can wait.

Those dishes can wait, says Princess.

No, Doctor says, *they cannot.*

Yes, she says, *just a few minutes. Just a few more minutes while I finish this sky*. Brushes sienna onto the palette, hums under her breath, a little song about rain. *Rain, rain, go away*, she hums silently, rubbing sienna on her canvas. *Little Princess wants to . . .*

Now!

The paint tube skips from her hand. She leans down to pick it up, but his heavy shoe stops her. Sienna bursts under her palm and spreads sickeningly, oozing up in-between her fingers.

Now look what you did, he says.

I didn't.

You will have to clean that up. Yes you will. You will have to lick it up off the floor.

I will not.

Bitch!

And then, slowly, she leans down, tongue prepared.

On your knees, he says. *You will learn just exactly who you are.*

Rita is no creative writer, she's a *journalist.* Any other writing is a waste of her time. But Creative Writing is in her curriculum, so she has to take it.

Then she meets Charlotte and Rita falls. Wildly and head-over-heels into love. Finds excuses to stay after class. Excuses to visit Charlotte's office. Excuses to run into Charlotte.

Writes like mad, a short story about woman-love, for her second Charlotte assignment.

"It's a good story," Charlotte says.

"Why did you give me a 'C' then?" asks Rita. "If it's such a good story."

"It isn't believable," says Charlotte. "It's stilted. The way this woman, 'Lisa'?, follows around after 'Selma', it just isn't realistic. And the way you say they make love . . . I wonder, have you ever made love with a woman?"

Rita blushes deep rose and picks at her shirt cuff, the shirt under which she is naked for Charlotte.

"You don't have to say," says Charlotte gently.

Rita coughs abruptly. "Well, I *have*. A lot."

Suddenly Charlotte is kissing Rita's mouth, her tongue is inside Rita's mouth, and Rita is kissing back.

The 'C' story slides off Charlotte's lap and scatters.

"What is it you know about love with a *real* woman?" she whispers.

Rita's mouth is on fire, singed from that kiss.

"Nothing," she mutters, truth after all.

Charlotte's hand inches up along Rita's thigh. "I shouldn't do this."

Rita's heart crumples a bit. Why is it everyone always says that?

Crushes her fingers against Charlotte's, urging her further.

Charlotte touches Rita's left nipple under her shirt where she is bare, where her nipples are fat from lust. Rita says nothing while Charlotte rims her lips around that erect nipple.

Who could write this? There are no words for this, she thinks later, there are no fucking words.

Charlotte stands by the green chalkboard. The shoulders of her soft rose suit are brushed with chalk dust. Dust shivers in the room.

Rita is front-row-centre, memorizing the shape of Charlotte's right eyebrow.

Charlotte sees, nods, just for Rita.

Rita twists her lips, leans back in her chair, and stretches one bare leg towards teacher. Grins.

Charlotte nods again. Dismisses the rest of the class. Chairs scrape, twenty voices hum.

"Rita," she says. "Stay after."

Waits behind Simon, anxious Simon, always with some question. Waits her turn for Charlotte. He is finished finally, asks Rita to come for coffee.

"Not now," she says, impatient.

Charlotte arranges papers in her briefcase, one at a time.

Rita steps behind her where she cannot be seen from the doorway. Slides one hand under Charlotte's skirt. Lips on Charlotte's earlobe, teacher's pussy under her fingers.

"No Rita," says Charlotte, rubbing honey onto Rita's palm.

"For later," laughs Rita, "so I can smell it all afternoon."

Husband answers the phone and Rita's heart sinks right into the ragged soles of her red sneakers.

Go away, she thinks.

Yesterday's lettuce is frozen soggy in her fridge; the thermostat was set at six. She thought that was normal, but it turned out she was wrong.

Husband, at home, in Charlotte's kitchen. She says he's a *great cook*.

Rita doesn't cook, can't get to Charlotte through food like Husband can. Takes her out for dinner when she sells a story, or when Daddy sends extra money.

But in Rita's kitchen, breakfast is always the same. Cereal from boxes. Toast, usually burnt.

Charlotte only stays for breakfast when she's still dripping, when she wants more from Rita. Otherwise she goes home to Husband and omelette, soufflé, waffles.

She says she likes Husband in the kitchen, and in bed too.

"More than me?" Rita asks.

"Different," is all Charlotte will give.

"That's a meaningless term," says Rita-the-reporter.

"To you," Charlotte says, and that is that.

Charlotte's husband and Rita sit across the table from Charlotte. Eating rich food made by Husband.

He's crazy, Rita thinks. *Crazy about Charlotte. This table is rife with people who are crazy about Charlotte.*

Charlotte is animated, inflamed by candlelight and Sylvia Plath.

Neither Husband nor Rita give one shit about Plath. All they give a shit about is Charlotte, who does give a shit about Plath. Charlotte talks on and on about Plath, *poor old Plath inside her Bell Jar*. Then she talks about the sauce He has made *to perfection*. Then she talks about Plath some more.

All that matters is that she is talking. Rita would trudge through manure, barefoot through glass. Would follow her honey-drenched voice anywhere.

Honey drips from Charlotte's tongue into the candle flame where it sputters and steams like sweet incense.

Charlotte curls her tongue around that flame. Licks at it, laps it up. She is on fire from the inside out.

Rita swallows quickly, sucks back the urge to get that honey from her tongue.

Husband's hand rests suddenly on Rita's bare knee, fingers coax themselves around her skin. Rita looks down, then back up at Charlotte whose silver tongue flickers.

"Why are you doing that?" asks Rita hoarsely.

Husband's hand vanishes as quickly as it appeared.

Charlotte goes on dripping honey from her mouth.

Sage skips classes to party, or because she's hung-over, or because she worked late. In heat all the time. A different guy in her bed almost every night.

Forgets to change her sheets, do her laundry. Forgets to pay her phone bill. Can't remember the name of the guy she wakes up with.

She's having a great time.

Charlotte spills herself all over Rita without shame, but she keeps Rita secret.

She says she could lose *it all, job, marriage, the life* she has *worked so hard to get.*

Says Rita could lose *it all* too.

"You've never even had a boyfriend," she tells her.

Rita is dumb with Charlotte, accepting any little crumb that she can get.

Spends a lot of time waiting for crumbs from Charlotte.

In Rita's two-room apartment, Charlotte gets rough.

"You sicken me!" she screams. Crumples the paper Rita wrote about city council, about women on city council, in Rita's face. "How can you write such drivel? How dare you call yourself a writer!"

Tapered white fingers rip at Rita's little story. Toss the shreds at Rita, still naked, still in bed after being loved by Charlotte.

Charlotte grapples with her soft-as-a-glove Italian leather briefcase, pulls out some paper.

"Now *this*," she says, "this is a story. If you, Rita, had *half* the talent Drew has . . . What you are doing is wasting your time. Worse still, you waste *my* time, Rita."

Charlotte's words rip into Rita's heart like shards of glass.

Her body gets cold. She reaches for her shirt from the heap of their clothing on the floor beside the bed, slides one arm slowly into one sleeve. That familiar ice is filling her up again.

It will remain inside no matter how many layers of clothing cover her.

Charlotte is screaming again, flooding the air in Rita's apartment with her rage.

Nails claw at Rita's skin. That ice swells in her belly.

But Rita does not hit back.

Nothing else matters when Charlotte touches her.

So Rita does her best to cover all those bruises.

Charlotte shreds her face; she goes into hiding.

Lets her hair grow longer for a veil to hide behind.

"I can't help myself," Rita tells Sage over beer. "I love her."

"I don't give a shit," says Sage. "You can't let her keep fucking you over. No matter how much you think you love her. Why does she do it?"

"I'm just an easy target."

"Maybe it's that jealousy of yours."

"But I let her have it all. I keep all her secrets."

"Maybe she's worried you'll tell."

"She says she loves her husband."

"She says she loves you, too. What do *you* get out of it?"

"Charlotte."

"Who hits you. Who makes you be her dirty little secret."

"Do you think it's because of my jealousy?"

"You don't beat someone like that because of jealousy," says Sage. "It's just sick."

"She says they're all better than me."

Rita's back hurts where welts left by Charlotte's rings are weeping. She drinks her beer quickly to help swallow the lump deep in her throat.

At Sage's place there's room for Rita. Room in the bed, room on the pull-out couch. Room on the floor. Tonight, there's room all over for Rita.

Charlotte tells Drew to stay after Creative Writing class.

Rita hears; she stays too.

"Rita," says Charlotte, "I need to talk to Drew."

"*I* need to talk to *you*," says Rita.

"Later. In my office."

Drew is gazing at Charlotte with smitten eyes. She gazes back at Drew.

Rita paces around Charlotte's office, reads press releases about writing contests on the walls, and waits and waits until she is late for class and has to go.

Leaves an unsigned note, no evidence.

Fresh shame fills her.

20

Rita struggles with her backpack, searching for her keys. Jumps when Sage steps up behind her.

"I didn't see you," says Rita.

"I've been waiting. I was starting to think you'd never get here. It's fucking cold out here."

"It's December," says Rita. "What do you expect?"

"Do you have your keys? The outside door is locked."

Rita gives her backpack to Sage to hold while she digs inside.

"What the hell have you got in here? It weighs a ton."

"Shut that door behind you. The caretaker says bums come inside to sleep. We have to keep that door locked."

"These stairs are creepy. Don't you get scared?"

"Not of stairs," says Rita.

"Anything could be lurking around these corners," says Sage, peering around nervously. "I'd hate it."

"Lucky you don't have to live here."

Rita unlocks her apartment door, lets Sage in ahead.

Sage drops the bag on the floor.

"I'm glad I'm not taking Journalism."

"If you did any work, you'd have stuff to lug around too. Should I make coffee?"

"Have you got any booze?"

"I hardly ever drink."

"If you have money, we could get some."

"What happened to your job?"

"I had to pay my student fees. They were threatening to kick me out."

"Can't Lorraine help you out?"

"Not fucking likely. She sends all her money to that asshole. All he has to do is phone."

Rita unfolds a filter. "I guess this means you can't pay me back that damage deposit you still owe me."

Sage throws her parka on the floor by the bookbag, and flops into Rita's only armchair.

"I'm broke. Are we going to be as gullible as Lorraine when we get old?"

"I am already," Rita says, pouring water into her coffee maker.

"Which is why you're gonna buy the booze for us tonight."

"I have homework to do. I've got classes tomorrow."

"I'm lonely."

"You're not even alone, you're with me."

"That's why I'm here. I took the chance that bitch wouldn't be around."

"What happened to Shane?"

"He got back together with what's-her-face," Sage says, staring at her feet. "I need some new winter boots."

"You want me to get you boots?" Rita fills two mugs. "Here's your coffee."

"Bring it here. I don't wanna move."

"Get it yourself. I'm leaving next weekend for the Christmas break. Do you want a ride or are you taking the bus?"

"I've got shifts scheduled."

"Aren't you going home for Christmas?"

"Lorraine isn't big on Christmas. What's happening with you and Charlotte?"

Rita yawns. "I'm so *tired,*" she says.

"Of Charlotte?"

"Just tired. Of everything."

"Is she still jerking you around?"

"It's been better lately."

"What does that mean? Is she still hitting you?"

"She hasn't for a while."

"Did you tell her to fuck off?"

"She told me she's sorry and that she doesn't know why she does it. She says she gets frustrated."

Sage stirs her coffee with her finger, then licks the finger.

"Does that mean she's going to stop?"

"All I know is what she said."

"Can I stay here tonight?"

"I don't think so. Charlotte might find out."

"Big deal. She fucks her husband, doesn't she?"

"That's different." Rita shrugs. "She might find out."

"Who's going to tell?"

Sage finishes the beer she coaxed Rita into buying. Rita, bent over a book, is studying. Sage sees the ragged edges of a scar under Rita's collar when she leans forward.

She sets down her empty bottle with the label half scratched off.

"Rags, should I leave now?"

When Rita looks up, the scar vanishes.

"You don't have to go," she says softly.

"What if Charlotte finds out?"

"Who'd tell her?"

Rita drives home alone.

Sage says she's skipping Christmas.

"I can make tons of tips during the holidays," she says.

Shane and his other girlfriend have split up again.

Sage with Shane, Charlotte with husband, a Canadian Lit assignment due January second.

Snow drifts lightly across the Trans Canada.

Vivaldi on the radio.

The house is lit up; there's a tree in the front window.

Timmy meets her at the door.

"There you are. Mom! Rags is home!"

"Where is she?" asks Rita.

"Come look at the tree," Timmy says.

"Nice tree. Did you help with the decorating?"

"I did most of it," he says. "This present's for you."

"You're not supposed to shake it. It could break. Where's Mom?"

"Making supper. We'll eat when Dad comes and then we'll open our presents."

Rita drags her books and suitcase up the stairs to her room. She stays there until she hears her dad's car outside.

"Rags is home!" she hears Timmy say.

Her two silent parents with bowed heads at the Christmas table while her father prays a grace.

Raymond, with his quiet girlfriend Tina; sullen Danny, with nothing to say; Rita, who thinks too much.

Timmy's head is up; he winks at her.

Her brothers chorus *amen*, then they all dig in to dinner.

Manma's in her old rocking chair by the big kitchen window.

Coloured lights edge the eaves of the houses on Elm Street.

Families with subdued eager children gather.

Choirs in churches.

Fathers and daughters.

Katie.

Sage works the evening shift.

Serving city people eating pizza and drinking beer on Christmas eve.

Calls Lorraine early Christmas morning.

"Hi, Maw. Merry Ho Ho."

"I wish you were home," says Lorraine.

"Did you get the card?"

"And the bracelet. You shouldn't have spent so much."

"Aw hell. I love the stuff you sent too."

Christmas on the coast. Pearce hangs out at the gay bar with her buddy Alfred. A bunch of fags without families.

There's way too much tinsel.

Alfred and his friends in drag.

"If Mama could see me now! Woo-whee!" he chortles, eyes bright from the lines of coke and doing each other in the back rooms.

Pearce's headache worsens as the time stretches.

At dawn she calls a cab.

The old man is on his annual holiday drunk.

Halfway through his booze, he gets noisy.

"That fuckin' cunt mother of yours," he roars. "Why'd she have ta go an' leave?"

"She died, Dad," Eddie says. "She didn't do it on purpose."

"Never trust a fuckin' dame," says his dad. "Let that be a lesson."

Eddie covers his dad's butt at the store.

There's not much of Christmas to be had.

Rita sees Eddie once.

He tells her about the lumber store. Says nothing about his father.

She talks about school. Says nothing about Charlotte.

There's a wall of stone between them.

21

"Happy New Year!" Rita sings to herself at midnight, raising her coffee mug.

Then she returns to the homework spread out over her floor.

Charlotte invites Rita for dinner after New Year's.

Tells her what to wear and how to do her hair and how she should behave. Charlotte's satisfaction is something to work hard for these days.

Dinner with Husband.

"Please don't make me sit beside him," begs Rita.

Charlotte is animated, and Husband touches her a lot while Rita squirms inside.

They go to the living room after dinner, a room for an architecture magazine, filled with sculptures made by Husband.

He pours drinks, lights a hash pipe, and passes it to Rita. She smokes, admires his sculpture, smokes.

Charlotte drinks. Scotch with a bit of ice.

"Rita," she says, stretching lazily through the haze, "come up to the loft with me."

Rita follows, leaving Husband sucking on the pipe in a cloud.

The sculpture in the loft bedroom is of Charlotte. It is naked, and bent down from the waist so the real Charlotte can set her drink on its butt. Rita draws her finger down the crack in the sculpture's buttocks and the real Charlotte nuzzles her neck.

Rita giggles. *Two Charlottes, one in front, one behind.* The live

Charlotte runs her hand down her back and then she is being undressed.

She's naked underneath her dress, according to instruction. The bruises from last time are faded and dull, and nearly match her regular skin.

"What about *him*?" she whispers.

"Never mind about him," says Charlotte, pressing her down onto the bed.

Rita shuts her eyes, feeling Charlotte's tongue.

Opens them. Husband. Beside her, petting himself.

Charlotte laughs through her teeth wrapped gently around Rita's clit.

Husband's breath is hot. He touches at her with both his hands, rubs himself against her skin.

"*No!*" says Rita loudly.

Charlotte raises her head.

"I say *yes*," she says, her voice hard.

Rita crumbles.

Charlotte positions herself over her face. She's pressed against Rita's mouth now and there is no room for any sound.

Husband pushes inside where Charlotte's tongue has moistened.

His flesh hurts more. More than the ring welts, more than the screaming and the bruising of Charlotte's rage. He rolls off easily when he's finished, and Charlotte takes his place again with her efficient mouth.

But Rita has gone numb.

She stares silently out the car window.

Charlotte reaches across to open the door from the inside.

"I love you, Rita," she says.

Rita has forgotten how to echo.

"Thanks for *everything*. You saved my life tonight."

"You owe me," Rita says dully.

Shoves the car door open.

Then she stands, watching Charlotte's car disappear like a pumpkin coach into midnight.

Rita wishes everything away.

Saturday passes. Like some slow-moving snail at the bottom of an aquarium.

The phone starts ringing at five-thirty and doesn't stop ringing until twelve-forty.

Rita sleeps like a snarled Slinky, caught in her own coils.

Sunday she wakes up too early, with the day stretching ahead of her like infinity.

Cleans the apartment. Packs clothing she no longer wants, to give away. Everything she has ever worn for Charlotte, until the only things left in her closet are a few pair of jeans and some ragged sneakers.

She studies her face in the bathroom mirror; it seems long. This hair is all wrong.

Rita finds her paste-up shears and begins to saw at Charlotte's hair. While she's hacking at the dead hair, the phone begins ringing again.

Keeps ringing while she steams her new scalp in the shower, while she rubs off old skin; ringing while she inspects her body for new bruises under the bare bathroom light bulb. While she says goodbye to Charlotte's angry touching.

Keeps ringing while she shreds Charlotte's copies of Plath into the kitchen garbage with the other garbage: used coffee grinds, eggshells, and orange peels.

Monday there is no Creative Writing class, and Rita buries herself in digging out someone else's story.

She and her project partner Sandy celebrate her first-ever *no comment* by going out for beer.

Unplugs her phone when she gets home.

Tuesday Rita skips out. It's a Creative Writing day.

Wednesday she and Sandy smoke up during their lunch break, and then giggle together through their afternoon Television class.

Thursday and Rita has managed to avoid Charlotte all week.

But when she reaches the landing by her apartment, there she is. Charlotte, with an armful of red roses and a big smile.

"What happened to your hair?"

"What are *you* doing here?"

"I've missed you. I haven't seen you all week."

"So?"

"Can we go in? You know how much I hate standing out here."

Rita's heart pounds like a drum.

"No," she says.

"Well, I do," says Charlotte.

"No," Rita says again.

"I brought wine."

Her fine leather boot toe taps the brown paper sack leaned against Rita's door.

"I can do better without your games."

"What games?" asks Charlotte, lifting her shaped eyebrows.

"Take your fucking flowers and your stinking dry white."

Charlotte picks up the paper sack, raises her hand above her shoulder, and fires.

Rita ducks.

Shattering glass and wine spray the wall, and the soggy bag crumples to the floor.

Charlotte kicks at the dropped roses.

"You'll regret this!"

"Why don't you at least clean up your mess?" shouts Rita.

But Charlotte is already vanishing gracefully down the dingy stairs.

Shane catches Sage before she falls off the bar stool.

"Good thing you're here. I could've hurt myself."

"Let's go outside, get some air," he says.

"There's no air out there," says Sage, but follows him anyway.

"Let's walk."

"Uh-oh. I'm in some kinda shit now."

"It's time for us to call it quits," Shane says.

"You're back with what's-her-name."

"Yeah. You got it."

"I don't know if I can make it home by myself," says Sage. "Will you walk me?"

Another Sunday, damp and grey and leaking.

Rita wraps herself up in the rusty red quilt she bought for fifty cents at the thrift shop on the corner, and stares out at the sky, the street, the rain.

Her Creative Writing assignment lies on the floor.

She has avoided Charlotte's class, has avoided having to look at Charlotte, but she still has to do the work. At least Charlotte isn't failing her. She passes, barely, just as before.

Rita leaps from her window-watch when the door buzzes.

"Am I ever glad to see you!" she says even before she sees Sage.

"Are you alone?"

"Am I ever."

Sage shrugs out of her soaked denim jacket and slumps into Rita's armchair. Her only armchair. Rita sits on a cushion on the floor.

"I'm depressed," sighs Sage.

"So am I."

"It's fucking Sunday."

"It's raining."

"We could rent a video."

"Make popcorn."

"I'm the expert."

"What movie should we get?"

"Something hot."

"You know I don't have a television."

"Shit. And my place is out. Randi's got some guy over there. She's on a marathon."

"I broke off with Charlotte."

"I like your hair," grins Sage.

"We'll order pizza, and just talk," says Rita happily.

"I'm broke."

"You're always broke. My dad sent a cheque on Friday. He said, *Do something special.*"

"I got dumped by Shane again."

"Good thing you've got me, then."

"Have I?"

Rita leans slowly back until her head rests between Sage's thighs.

"You know it!"

22

Daddy calls.

"I tried to phone yesterday," he says. "I thought we could go out."

"I have tons of work, but I can put it off."

"I'm here right now with a . . . friend . . . who happens to live really close to your place."

"You don't have to tell me," says Rita quickly.

"There's someone I want you to meet."

"No, Daddy! Don't . . . "

"I'm bringing her. We'll be over in ten minutes."

"I'll be downstairs so you won't have to wait."

Peering through the security door into winter dusk, watching for her father's LTD Wagon.

A blonde in a red Camaro pulls to the curb, stops, honks.

Rita's dad beams through the passenger window, waves.

"In here!" he shouts.

Holds open his door for Rita to climb into the back seat.

"Nancy, this is my daughter Rita. Rita, Nancy."

The blonde nods. "Hi there!"

"Hi, Dad," says Rita. "I didn't recognize this car."

"I forgot to tell you about the car," says her father. "Nancy is the friend I want you to meet."

"Is this your car, Dad?"

"It's mine," says the blonde.

"Where are we going?"

"The Steak House," says Nancy. "Do you eat red meat? It's okay if you don't. There's lobster and shrimp . . . "

"That's fine," Rita says. "I'll be fine."

Dinner is formal with dressed waiters, wine-tasting, and *how would you like your steak?*

Rita orders shrimp.

The blonde touches her father often — his arm, his hand, his thigh.

Rita can't place her face on top of that body in the photographs she spied on. *Maybe that was a different one.*

"How's Mom?" Rita asks, after choosing from the dessert cart.

"To the point," laughs Nancy.

"The same," her father says.

"Who's at the store? Raymond?"

"He's taking it over," her father says. "He's a big boy now, he's getting married this summer."

"To whom?"

"Tina."

"Poor Tina."

"They've been dating since high school. It's time, it's what's done."

"Is she pregnant?" asks Rita. "The way I see it, *that's* what's mostly done."

"How are your classes?" Nancy asks. "I understand you're taking journalism."

"You wouldn't believe the work! I don't have time for anything else."

"Are you seeing someone?" asks her father.

"I was. It's over."

"Where's Sage living now?"

"She's sharing an apartment and she's waitressing part-time."

"Is Lorraine helping her out?"

"No. Can you give me a few bucks, Dad?"

"I've got a cheque for you. How are your grades?"

"Honours."

"She's the smart one," he tells Nancy, handing the cheque to Rita.

Nancy smiles, brushes at his hand with hers. "Are you going to tell her, or should I?" she asks.

Her father straightens in his chair. "Rita," he says.

"Please don't . . . " Rita says.

"I have to. Nancy and I are going to be living together."

"Daddy . . . "

"We've known each other for years," says Nancy.

"Raymond's taking over the store, and I'm moving to the city to live. With Nancy."

"What about Mom?"

"Nancy's a pharmacist."

"What about Mom?"

"I'm opening the franchise here. I've been working on it for two years."

"Mom is sick!" says Rita. "Daddy, Mom is . . . "

"I can't help that."

"You could do *something*!"

"What?" her father asks, spreading his hands, palms upward.

"I don't know!" shouts Rita. "I'm just her kid!"

"Well, neither do I," her father says quietly.

"There are some things you don't understand," says Nancy.

"And you do? You're his fucking mistress."

"Rita!"

"Everyone in town knows," says Rita. "Even Mom knows, she told me."

"I hoped you were old enough now," says her father. "Besides, you've never been a saint yourself. Talking about what *everyone in town knows*."

"Like what?" asks Rita coldly.

"I don't want to get into this," her father says, helplessly.

"Your lifestyle," says Nancy softly, looking around.

Rita stares grimly at Nancy, daring, heart pounding fiercely.

"*Lifestyle,*" she repeats.

"Apparently," says Nancy, looking at Rita's father, "you find girls attractive."

"And," her father adds, "I've been helping to support that lover of yours without a word. I think that should count for something, don't you? I've gone to bat for you, Rita."

"*Girls,*" says Rita.

"Women, then," Nancy says. "Your lifestyle is your own concern, but your father has defended you, and now you're like this . . . judgmental. I didn't expect it."

"Defended me when? Against what?"

"Rumours and innuendo. Your mother. Your own brothers. Businessmen I've had to deal with."

"My mother?"

"She doesn't understand. Thinks it's something she's done wrong to make you this way."

Rita slides her plate of mangled chocolate further away, digs into her pocket.

"I need to smoke."

"So do I," says Nancy with relief.

Rita lights Nancy's cigarette first.

"What you want from me, then . . . "

"Just your acceptance," says Nancy.

"And support," says her father.

Rita drags herself out of bed at six o'clock the next morning to finish her homework.

Acceptance and support.

What about *love*?

She cashes his cheque. Deposits seven hundred to savings for rent and utilities, and keeps a few hundred to spend.

Finds a crystal unicorn for her mom to add to her collection. Buys it.

A bottle of Sage's favourite perfume.

A case of import beer.

A sexy teddy for herself and some typing ribbons.

Lays her treasure on her bed and calls Sage.

"Let me take you out," she says.

"My dad's moving in with his mistress."

"Hey, keen."

"They want my *acceptance and support*. I guess they want me to be on their side."

"Who's on the other side?"

"Dad says he stuck up for me in town. He says everyone knows about my *lifestyle*."

"You mean liking girls?"

"That's what he said," shrugs Rita.

"Stuck up for you?"

"He said my mom thinks it's her fault that I'm this way."

"In psychology," Sage says, "we learned about what makes guys gay: an overbearing mother and an absent father. But they don't say anything about girls. Maybe it's the opposite."

"My father's not exactly overbearing. And mom was there all the time, raising us."

"Some people say it's just the way you're born. Something to do with chromosomes — too many X's and not enough Y's or something. But they always just talk about guys."

"Same as with everything else."

"Why do *you* think you turned out this way?"

"It's always been like this. When I look around," she says, "all I really see is the women."

Sage grins. "I see everyone. That's *my* problem."

Sage's new roommate Randi used to sleep with Joey who used to sleep with Sage, and who got the two of them together.

Neither of them sleep with Joey now, but he uses their couch when it suits him.

Randi slings beer at the Zoo until closing time, then brings drunks back to their place to screw or smoke or fight. She plays hard rock on her stereo all night long so loud they can't hear if neighbours are banging on floors.

Now she's got a new boyfriend, the same one for over a week.

"What are you still doing with this guy?" asks Sage.

"It's been slim pickin's at the Zoo lately," says Randi. "Those university guys are droppin' away like flies."

"They're all studying for mid-terms."

"I never see *you* crackin' the books."

"There isn't any time," says Sage. "Between work at night and classes all day."

"When's the last time you went to a fuckin' class?"

"I sleep in," says Sage. "I forget."

"So long's you keep payin' your half of the rent on this hole, I don't give a shit. It sure the fuck don't matter to me."

"We want Timmy," Nancy says firmly. "We're going for full custody."

"You can't just waltz in and take him away. He's lived there all his life. Nothing's changed for him. Daddy was never really there anyway."

"Rita," says Nancy in her superior tone, "your mother is very sick. She can't take proper care of that ten-year-old."

"She's managed so far."

"He's a bright kid," Nancy says, swinging her blonde hair back over her shoulders. "*Despite* her, and he deserves more. Your dad and I will give him private school, tutors, the best."

"There's something about what you just said," says Rita slowly. "I can't quite put my finger on it but . . . and what about Danny?"

"You know I'm right," says Nancy, getting up. "I have to get back to work now. We'll talk more later."

Now her father is coming over. To talk. Without Nancy.

Makes coffee. Buzzes him through the security door. Hangs his jacket on the coat tree.

"You've lost weight, Daddy," she says.

"Just a few extra pounds."

She offers him her only chair.

"Nice little place," he observes. "But you need more furniture."

"What for?" asks Rita.

"For guests," he says. "And a television."

"I don't have guests."

She gets coffee, then sits cross-legged on her floor cushion.

"Where do you do your school work? You don't even have a desk."

"I work on the floor. It's comfortable."

He sips, stirs, sips again.

"Isn't there enough sugar? I can get more."

"No, this is fine. Nancy said she talked to you about custody."

"She talked. And I listened."

"She said you weren't very supportive," says her father, setting the cup on the floor.

"What did you expect? I don't think it's fair."

"Why not?"

"Because he's with Mom. Because that's his home. Because you and Nancy are strangers to him," says Rita, ticking off her three *becauses* on her fingers.

"I'm his *father*! I understood we could count on you to be supportive."

"There's that word again. Does it just mean my blanket approval to anything you two decide that you want from me?"

He picks up his coffee, sets it back down.

"I've told you what I think of some of your choices, and how I've supported you regardless. Now it's your turn."

"I don't know," she says slowly, "if that's exactly fair either."

"I've been wanting to ask you something," her father says, holding his cup tightly.

"What?" asks Rita, leaning back against the wall.

"What is it that I did to you?"

"Did?"

"To make you this way. Did I hurt you? Is there anything I could have done differently?"

"Not hurt. Done differently? Well, yeah, there's a lot of stuff you didn't do that you could've done."

"To make you want to be with men."

"Ah."

"It's just that you've chosen this . . . lifestyle . . . that excludes men," he says, clearing his throat. "It makes me wonder."

"Daddy," says Rita. "Nothing I choose has anything to do with anything you did, or didn't, do."

"Good," he says heartily.

"I just don't want to have sex with men."

"Have you ever tried?"

"Tried?"

"With a man. I was thinking . . . if you tried it, you might like it. You might change your mind."

"I've tried, Daddy."

"You have?"

"I've done it, and it's been done to me."

"And you didn't . . . "

"It didn't make me want to change."

"Oh."

He sets down his cup again.

"Would you rather have a beer? I've got some, if you want."

"I could use a beer."

Rita gets up, gets a beer for her father.

"I'm sorry I don't have any glasses."

"I just don't understand."

"Understand what?"

He gulps half his beer.

"What is it that you *do*?" he asks at last.

"Do?"

"With girls."

Rita swallows. *What does he want?*

"What is it that *you* do?"

"Physiologically speaking," he says, "it's a little different."

"I'm speaking sexually," says Rita.

"Never mind," her father says quickly. "Forget I asked. It's none of my business."

"I'm sorry it's been so hard for you, my being different," Rita says carefully. "I never knew about that."

"We had trouble with Raymond, too. It's not just you."

"What kind of trouble?"

"Boy stuff," he says vaguely. "Nothing for you to worry about."

"What's going to happen to Timmy?"

"I'd like to get him away from that town. So he has a better chance."

"Because of private school?"

"Not just. Because you have to pay for who you are in that town. Who you're related to. And I want him to have more choices, not have to try so hard to live it all down."

"Okay," says Rita. "But what about Mom?"

23

"You're fucking Drew now," says Rita. "Aren't you?"

"That is none of your business," Charlotte says. "I think you should leave my office now."

"Is there anyone you won't fuck? Don't you have any standards at all?"

"Rita, don't make this ugly."

"I *could* scream. I wonder who'd hear."

"I have a lot of good friends in high places."

"No doubt. But you're fucking with your students, come on! I'm going to tell Drew about you."

"You have no influence over Drew," says Charlotte coldly. "He's got his own mind."

"Maybe. But he's a minor. Even *you* know what that means. Are you beating on him too, or was it just me?"

"I don't know what you're talking about."

"For a tough broad, you can be awfully dumb."

"After all, there are no witnesses. You say one thing, I say another. Who are people going to believe?"

Rita retreats to her apartment.

Spreads out all her assignments and surveys the work she has to do.

Charlotte's face inside her head; Charlotte's lips forming words.

Who will people believe?

Rita picks up a textbook, drops it.

Walks angrily to her window and looks out at the city below.

Somewhere out there is Charlotte.

Maybe with Drew. Maybe with Husband. Maybe even with someone else.

Who knows *what* she's doing?

"Charlotte beat up on me all the time," Rita tells Drew.

"You're just jealous because you have a crush on her," he says. "I know all about it."

"Oh *man*," says Rita. "You're going to regret what you're doing."

Drew lays one of his soft, warm hands over hers on the table.

"I know how you feel," he says gently. "Because Charlotte's great. But she's not into women like you are. You should accept that."

Rita tugs her hand free.

"She and that husband of hers raped me."

"She said you'd say something like that. To get my attention."

"There's a statue of her in their loft, they have this canopy waterbed up there. Charlotte has a mole on her right thigh."

"You're not proving anything. Only your good imagination."

"I hope you like getting hurt, because that's what you're in for."

"Whatever," says Drew. "I'll get the bill for our coffee."

"Remember," Rita says, "I tried to warn you."

Drew is missing classes. Two days, then three.

Rita asks Sandy where he is.

Sandy shrugs.

"I haven't seen him around for a couple of days."

"I have this Current Events project with him, and I need to talk to him. Do you have his number?"

"Yeah, sure," says Sandy. "I'll get it for you."

"Can I talk to Drew?" Rita asks Drew's mother.

"Hi Charlotte," says Rita brightly. "How are you today?"

Charlotte looks up from the papers on her desk.

"Rita!" she says. "What a surprise!"

Rita closes the office door firmly, sits in the familiar red chair.

"Drew's jaw is broken. When your fucking husband raped him, he haemorrhaged. He's haemophiliac, he couldn't stop bleeding. His mom had to take him to Emergency."

Charlotte has gone chalk-white.

"They're pressing charges against you and that scum husband you pimp for," says Rita. "I warned you, he's just a kid. A rich white kid with parents who give a shit."

Charlotte is no longer watching Rita's mouth, she's reaching for her phone.

"Good idea," says Rita. "Call your fuckhead lawyer. Find out how much it'll cost you *now* to keep this job. And how much it'll cost to shut me up, because I intend to talk."

"If someone had warned you, would you have listened?" Drew asks.

Rita rakes her hair.

"I don't know," she says, finally.

"It's easy now," he says.

"Yeah," says Rita. "Looking back."

"My guess is that you wouldn't have listened either."

"You're probably right."

"You always think it's going to be different for you. I thought you were making it up because you were jealous of me with Charlotte."

"In a way, I was," says Rita. "I guess I loved her, despite everything. Or something."

"I did what I could."

"Will you have to go to court?"

"If it ever gets that far. Charlotte has a lot of friends in high places, and that asshole she's married to has money."

"It shouldn't make any difference," says Sage. "Money or not."

"Too bad, but it does."

"What about if you charge them, too?"

"I can't," says Rita. "I don't have rich parents who would stand beside me. It would kill my mother, and my father would hate it."

"At least they'll have to watch their steps now."

"At least. For a while," Rita says.

"I really don't want to go home right now."

"Why are you chewing at your nails?"

"I'm trying to cut down on smoking. Why did I ever start, anyway?"

Sage grins.

"Because of me."

Rita reaches for her cigarettes.

"Same reason I can't stop now."

"Lorraine wants me to be there. I booked off work and everything."

"You can always take the Greyhound."

"I hate the fucking Greyhound. I can't smoke."

"I don't want to face my mother," Rita says.

"Because of Nancy?"

"I'll have to pretend I don't know about Nancy. Or Timmy."

Rita sighs, stretches her bare toes.

"Maybe you can hide out with me at Lorraine's."

"Someone would tell my mother I was there."

"Lorraine wouldn't."

Rita wrinkles her forehead and rubs her fingertip along the lines.

"All this because *you* don't want to take a bus."

"Please," begs Sage.

Randi's having another serious relationship and Sage is marking days on the calendar.

"You're fucking them all."

"And you ain't fuckin' nobody," Randi says. "You *queer* or somethin'?"

"Just because I'm not some slut. What's *your* problem?"

"Back off. So what if I'm with him twenty-two days and three hours? What the fuck is that to you?"

Sage packs some clothes and visits Rita.

"Can I stay with you?" she asks. "I have to study somewhere and I can't do it there. She's got some guy there all the fucking time. I can't get any peace."

"You can stay," Rita says, "on one condition."

"That's your favourite word, isn't it?"

"On my terms. No guys. No parties."

"That's two. You said one."

"I said *on my terms*," Rita snaps. "That's one."

"Sex?"

"No sex."

"Not even with you?"

"*Especially* not with me," says Rita. "I have to pass my exams. I can't afford to screw up now."

Rita meets Susan in the school cafeteria. Bumps into her at the coffee bar, reaching for the real cream.

"That's no edible oil product," says Susan, grinning.

"It's not? I want my money back. I paid for edible oil."

Susan follows her to her seat.

"You're using the whole table. What're you studying?"

"Journalism. And I can't smoke, eat, or drink in the library. There's no one else here anyway, they're all in there."

"I was checking out admissions. I'm Susan."

"Rita. You want to get in here?"

"I'm applying for a job in the office."

"I'm studying for exams."

"What are you doing later?" asks Susan, flicking back a long, coppery braid.

"Studying," Rita says, watching Susan's eyes.

"After that?"

"Still studying," says Rita.

"When you're through studying, you wanna fuck?"

Rita calls her apartment from the pay phone in the cafeteria.

"You have to leave now," she tells Sage. "I'm bringing someone home."

***Leave,* she says.** Just like that. *You have to leave now.*

Sage phones the bus depot, then Lorraine.

"Mom," she says. "I'm coming home."

"What do they know about me?"

Susan just shrugs, laughs, kisses Rita's chin.

"I mean it. How should I act? What should I wear?"

"Who cares?"

Susan nuzzles Rita's nipple; it becomes erect for her mouth.

"Who cares about which?" Rita asks, shivering. "About them liking me, or what I should wear and how I should act?"

"Whether or not my parents like you won't make any difference to how I feel."

Rita fingers her hair, running through strands like orange thread.

"Ow! Don't tug."

Rita drops the hair.

"You don't have to stop. Just don't tug so hard."

"They'll think my hair is too short. Should I grow it out again?"

"Do *you* think your hair's too short?"

"It's easy like this."

"Okay then," says Susan.

Sinks her face into Rita's lap and that ends that.

Rita is on the ragged sofa in Susan's parents' family room, sharing a heavy, vinyl-covered photo album with Susan's mother.

"This is Giselle," says Susan's mother. "The first girlfriend Susan ever brought home."

Susan is in the kitchen, making punch for dinner.

"Moth-ther," she scolds.

"I don't mind," says Rita quickly. "I like looking at photos."

"She was so pretty," says Susan's mother wistfully. "Wasn't Giselle pretty?"

"Very pretty," Susan agrees. "Mom liked Giselle more than I did. Didn't you Mom?"

Rita tries to see her face, but she has turned towards the fridge and there is nothing to see.

Her mother flips the page.

"Caroline. Rod's girlfriend."

Susan emerges from the kitchen, wiping her hands on the tea towel draped over her right shoulder. "Caroline's okay," she says. " She's too good for *him*, anyway."

"Be sweet, Susan. Rod's a good boy. Have you got any brothers, Rita?"

"Three," says Rita.

"It's good for a girl to have brothers."

Rita shrugs.

"I suppose. I never liked it much."

"*Brothers,*" Susan says. Again, that rough edge.

"Brothers can be difficult too," says her mother.

Rita thinks about Raymond and nods.

"But having them can teach a girl what it is boys are like."

Rita nods again and glances at Susan.

"Truer words were never spoken," says Susan. "What boys are like, what they want, what they grow into."

"Not *all* men . . . " says her mother sharply.

"Let's please not start on this again. Not *all* men are trash. I know, you've told me. Over and over."

"There are good men and bad men, just as there are good and bad women."

"We can eat now. Should I call Daddy?" asks Susan.

"It smells great," Rita says. "I've never eaten a vegetarian meal before. I can hardly wait."

Susan goes to the bottom of the stairs.

"Daddy!" she shouts. "Dinner's ready!"

Her mother shuts the thick photo album, sets it with a thud on the glass-covered coffee table beside the sofa. Rises with effort.

"Come on then," she tells Rita. "Your chance to explore new culinary delights awaits you."

Obediently Rita rises and follows Susan's fat mother to the dining table.

24

Susan is baking up a storm in Rita's kitchen. Garlic bread made with yeast and lasagna from scratch.

Rita's at the table, doodling, watching Susan move like a whirlwind. All that kneading, mixing, boiling, and shredding.

"How did you decide you're lesbian?"

"It wasn't like I decided anything. I just was."

"I don't remember deciding either."

"But you said you did it with that guy in high school. Can you push back my hair?"

Rita sets down her pen.

"I love this hair of yours," she says, smoothing the loose ends inside a barrette at the nape of Susan's neck. "You never said if you've ever done it with a guy."

"There's nothing to tell."

She gets busy with lasagna cheeses and Rita returns to her chair perch.

"You've never done it with any guy?"

"Nothing that counts."

"Mine didn't count either," Rita says quickly.

"I had this aunt. She was killed a couple of years ago, murdered by a total stranger, for no reason. She was my favourite relative. I was about thirteen, and she was looking after me for the weekend while my parents went to some political convention, and I told her I never wanted to get married. She told me I didn't have to. *Look at me,* she said."

"Lucky you. I couldn't talk to anyone. Any grown-up, anyway. I could to Sage, but she kept trying to convince me that it didn't make any difference, girl or guy."

"My aunt," says Susan staring at the counter top piled with cheese she's shredded.

"How much cheese do you need?"

"That weekend my wonderful aunt, who I worshipped, crawled into my bed to *tuck me in* she said. I wanted to die."

"What?"

"My auntie," says Susan, still staring at her cheese mountain. "That was my first time with a woman."

Rita looks at Susan's back where the cords are clenching, at her bare, muscular arms.

She stands.

"Can I hug you now?" Rita asks softly.

"Yes." Susan's voice is small. "Please."

"I'm so sorry," Rita whispers into her silken hair. "It's not fair."

"No," Susan says. "Nothing is."

"Everything with your parents involves eating."

"My mother likes food. It's her greatest joy."

"I noticed. She's killing herself with it."

"I think that's the idea."

"Why does she want to kill herself?"

"I can think of a few good reasons," Susan says, waving her mascara brush. "Move over a bit, I can't see myself."

"I'm done anyway. There's not much more I can do with this face."

Susan's mother is bundled boldly into a pink taffeta cocktail dress which she says she made herself.

"She must've spent a fortune on the material," Rita whispers.

"Shh," says Susan. "You'll make me laugh."

"We can't have that. Laughing at a party, not in good taste."

Susan's mother deposits them in a room of older people. A woman Rita recognizes from the family photo album untangles herself from an older man who is busy trying to look down her bodice.

"Hi there! Long time no see," she tells Susan.

"Caroline!"

Caroline gives Rita a free peek down her bra when she pecks the air beside Susan's cheek.

Not bad, Rita thinks.

"And you must be Rita."

"Rita, this is Caroline. Rod's girlfriend."

Caroline grips Rita's upper arm.

She's leaving marks, Rita thinks, smiling stiffly.

"Hi," she says.

"You simply must come have a chat with me and tell me all about yourself. I've been dying to meet you. Rodney tells me you're a journalist. It must be so exciting."

Caroline pulls Rita with her to the bar.

"I'll have another," she tells the bartender. "And she'll have . . . what'll you have? White wine?"

"Maybe a beer," says Rita.

Caroline has stuck to her like lint to static. Rita allows it because she can see Susan is being kept busy greeting friends of her parents.

"Have you met Rodney yet? Oh, silly me! Of course not, or we'd have met too. Or at least I'd have heard about it."

"I've seen pictures. And Susan has mentioned him."

"I'll just bet she has!" titters Caroline. "Those two!" she says. "What a *pair*!"

"How do you mean?"

"Surely Susan's told you about her and Rodney. If I were the jealous type . . . Well, all I can say is, lucky for Rodney I'm not. I think it's just so kinky, it's cute."

Rita's stomach flips.

Pushes away from Caroline's painted toothy mouth.

Outside, Rita starts running. Runs until she can't run anymore. Runs as fast and as far from that house as she can, until there is no sound at all left inside her head except her own breathing.

"All of a sudden, you vanished," says Susan.

"I'm sorry." Rita picks up her brandy bottle.

"Why are you sitting here in the dark?"

"I intend to get drunk."

"You need it to be dark for that?"

"It's better that way."

"What the hell did Caroline *do*? May I sit here?"

"Sit wherever you want," says Rita.

Slumps further into the corner, away from Susan.

"Why don't you want me to touch you?"

"As usual," Rita says scornfully, "I can't find the fucking words. Some wordsmith, huh?"

"You want me to go?"

Rita winces. "I don't even know that. Part of me never wants to see you again. But another part thinks I'll die if you leave."

"I know that feeling," Susan says, leaning back against the wall beside Rita. "Maybe I'll just sit here for a while. And if you decide you want me to go, I'll go."

"I suppose . . . "

Rita stops, and drinks.

Susan stays silent, waiting.

"I guess this is just my stupid jealousy again," Rita says at last, "but why did you have to lie to me?"

When Susan leans forward, copper hair spirals down her back like a veil.

"What makes you think I lied? Something that Caroline said?"

"Caroline . . . "

"What did she tell you?"

"Never mind. I don't give a fuck. Not one fuck. Not at all."

Inside Rita then, something snaps.

Susan watches Rita sleeping, wrapped in moonlight.

Sooner or later, they make you pay for everything.

Daddy's home, she made him say.

"Say, *Naughty Mommy,*" she ordered him. "Say, *I see your pee-pee.*"

He said it and she rubbed his boy-palm across those smooth, puffy lips between her legs.

When he tugged away, she made him do it more.

Made him feel her good. Just like they showed her.

Susan's hair runs a twisted curtain across her face so Rita can't see her eyes.

"They made me sleep in their room. When they fucked, I woke up and it scared me. At first that's all it was, I think. Just happenstance. But later they got off on my being awake, of doing it in front of me. Then they started to include me. Touching me, putting me in between."

"How old were you?"

"It stopped after Rod was born. When I was five. That's when they moved me out of their room. You know the rest."

"I don't know what to say."

"Don't say anything," Susan says. "I can't bear it anyway."

Two in the morning.

Rita's buzzer is ringing.

Rita grunts.

"You want me to see what it is?"

Rita opens her eyes to take in the curve of Susan's hip, the red hair snaking down her back.

"Put on a shirt," she growls, shutting her eyes.

Then Susan is tugging on her jeans and hissing.

"It's your Dad! He says it's an emergency. He's coming up!"

Rita opens her eyes again.

"What the fuck time is it, anyway?" she asks, sitting up.

"Emergency!"

Slowly Rita drags a T-shirt over her head.

"Maybe Nancy kicked him out," she says loudly.

Her dad's voice. In the other room. "Where's Rita?"

"I'm coming, Dad! Just putting on my shirt."

"Rita!" calls Susan.

"Coming!"

Her father is standing by the window.

"Sit down," he says.

His face is greyer than his hair. Fuck, he's getting old.

"Maybe I should stand, so I don't fall asleep again."

"Sit *down*!" her father repeats, so Rita sits.

He kneels on the floor at her feet, takes her two hands in his. His grey face so close.

He's never been this close.

"I got a call," he says.

Behind her, Susan stands, resting her two hands on Rita's two shoulders.

Everyone is holding me. This should feel so good.

"About your mother."

Her father's lip quivers.

She notices grey nostril hair. *I didn't know they turned grey too.*

"She's dead." The quivering lip twists; tears fall from the grey eyes onto the greyer cheeks.

"Dead? Just like that . . . *dead*? Dead, how?"

"Too many *pills*," her crying father says. "Too many goddamn pills."

"She can't just go *dead* like that! It's not possible!" Rita screams into her grey father's face. "Let go of my fucking hands!"

Jumps from her chair, scattering their hands all around. Stomps across the room, to the window, to the fridge, to the door.

The grey man weeps aloud.

"Rita . . . " Susan says helplessly.

His crying floods the room.

Rita stops abruptly, turns. "Stop that crying, old man!" she screams. "You have *no* right!"

"I *loved* her," he whimpers.

"You lie," Rita says coldly.

"I loved her," he whispers into his hands.

Rita drops into the chair.

Her father's head falls onto her bare, bony knees and rests there.

She reaches out to touch his hair; she doesn't know why, it's just the way it's there. Like a broken baby doll, and she reaches out.

Susan's hands are on her shoulders, her lips against Rita's ear.

"Dead," says Rita.

25

There's a funeral to attend.

Rita hasn't ever been to a funeral. She has never had to help bury someone she knew. She never has had to help bury her own mother.

"I want to be a pallbearer," she tells her father.

"You can't," he says.

"Why the fuck not?"

"Only men are pallbearers."

"Is there any reason for that? You've got to have a penis to carry a casket?"

"That's just the way it's done. Are you going to fight me on this too?"

"Is Nancy coming?"

"Yes."

"I don't think she should," says Rita. "I don't think it's in *good taste*. She's your fucking mistress, it wouldn't look right."

"Are you trying to make a point here?"

"May I be a pallbearer for my mother?"

The stereo is cranked up as loud as Rita can stand. She and Sage are in her dead mother's living room painting their toe and fingernails black for the funeral. They bought the polish before they left the city.

Rita's dad and Nancy are driving out tomorrow with the boys, and Rita begged Sage to stay with her.

"It's too creepy. I keep thinking she's around the corner or in her bed or in the kitchen. I just know I'm going to see her here."

"Let's go to Lorraine's for night," Sage shouts above the music.

Rita turns down the volume.

"She'll be so pitying."

"She said to tell you you're welcome."

"I'd have to sleep alone. On that lumpy couch or something. I want to sleep with *you.*"

"Badly enough not to mind the ghosts?"

"I *need* to hold you."

"My nails are dry," says Sage. "Hold me now."

Rita shoves her hands up under Sage's sweatshirt.

"I want to feel your tits."

"There's ghosts in here," Sage mutters.

Rita tugs at Sage's shirt, twists it off over her head.

"Your nipples are so hard," she whispers.

"Yours too. It's in-fucking-decent."

Sage shoves her fresh black fingertips through Rita's satin funeral panties where Rita is already wet.

"Harder," says Rita.

"What about Susan?"

"I want to come with *you.*"

Sage takes off her glasses.

"Lie back," she says. "I need to taste you."

With a start, Rita awakens.

Sage is wrapped around her, breathing through her open mouth.

In my mother's house.

Moon spills through the window glass.

The travel alarm shows *three-forty.*

The house is stone silent. Except for Sage's raspy breathing and the ticking clock. Silent as stone.

Your mother was so very tired.

Rita shuts her eyes.

She needed to rest.

Her cheeks feel damp.

Fingers like a breeze caress her forehead, and Rita sleeps.

Rita is on one side, Raymond on the other. Their mother's casket in between.

This is the closest I ever want to get to you, brother. That thing about *death bringing people together*, it isn't true. When Raymond's hand brushes hers, she flinches. Tugs away. Can't meet his eyes.

Sage helps carry the coffin too, helps carry Rita's mother's body out of the church, and then out to the grave.

Her father with Nancy hanging off his arm.

We must be some sight.

Her father doesn't cry; he holds himself stiff and straight, holds Timmy by his side. Timmy whimpers, but that Danny is a cold one, *just like Raymond.*

Rita doesn't cry either.

When the first shovelful of dirt drops on the casket, she walks away.

It's what she wanted, Rita tells herself.

Eddie, from the gravesite, is running after her.

"It was nice of you to come, Eddie."

"I came to see *you.*"

"You didn't even know my mother."

Eddie falls in step beside her.

"Nobody did," he says.

"Her parents died in that accident when she was little. I didn't even know till today. She never talked to me."

"May I hold your hand?"

"I don't even know if I'll miss her. It seems like she was never really there."

"It was different to see female pallbearers."

"I was just supposed to sit there while Raymond did the carrying."

Eddie points at a park bench.

"Let's stop here."

"I think she got what she wanted," says Rita softly.

"Maybe it was her only option."

"Maybe."

"You know what I want?"

"To get out of here."

"Even more than that."

"More than that?"

"To marry you."

A soft panic flutters inside Rita.

"Oh, *no*!" she protests. "You don't want that. Really, Eddie."

"That *is* what I want," says Eddie, studying his shoes. "I can't stop thinking about it."

"But you know I can't."

"You did it with me once. You *choose* not to. You could change."

"I *could* be half-a-person, dead inside, like her. Stoned all the time, just to get through my life."

"What the hell have *women* ever done for you?"

Without another word, Rita gets up and stalks away, head held high.

"Wait up!" he shouts, but Rita just keeps walking. Faster.

Now you've done it, idiot. She doesn't want to hear it. Think about it: this is a difference too wide to span with silly words.

Sage pulls down the rear-view mirror to admire the ash-white highlights she got Lorraine to put in her hair.

"It looks like you're going grey," says Rita.

"Guys go nuts for blonde."

"Nancy's blonde."

"So's your dad," says Sage, flipping up the mirror. "So are your brothers. Why aren't you?"

"Maybe my mom had her own fling. This is your building, right?"

"I wonder who Randi's doing now. Don't start obsessing about this shit. Call me."

Rita chews through the stack of crosswords she's been clipping from weekend papers for months.

Tells Susan she's not ready to see her yet.

Gnaws at her black polish, smokes cigarettes, and does those puzzles.

On the third day she phones Susan back, her voice husky from smoking and no sleep.

Tells her to pick up her things at four-fifteen.

"I won't be here," she says. "Use your keys and leave them on the table when you're done."

"What did I do?"

"You have garbage in your spirit. Dump it."

"You're right about that," Susan says. "But I do love you. Not that I know what that means."

Calls her father but Nancy answers.

"I don't think you should talk to Timmy right now. He's just getting used to us. It'd only confuse him more."

"Is it your decision to make?"

"I'm his only mother now."

Rita imagines Nancy swinging her long blonde hair.

"I'm not going to finish school."

"She's dead and buried. Get on with your own life."

"This *is* my own life," Rita says. "What*ever* I plan to do with it."

"What does Susan say about this?" asks Sage, rubbing her hands together briskly. She tugs her sweatshirt sleeves down over her knuckles. "Fuck man, aren't you cold?"

"Susan has some shit she has to work through."

"*Shit.*"

"From when she was a kid."

"Has she moved out?"

"I told her to. *Leave*, I said, *you have garbage in your spirit. Dump it.*"

"She fell for that?"

"She knows I'm right."

"Everyone knows you're always right," Sage says glumly. "It's way too fucking cold. Let's walk, at least."

Rita gets up from the park bench where they've been sitting. "Come on, then."

"You dumped her because she's got *garbage in her spirit*. Not because of your mother."

"Nothing whatsoever to do with that. Whatso*fucking*ever."

"If you don't finish school," says Sage through chattering teeth, "what will you do? You want to be a journalist more than anything."

"I'll *be* a journalist."

"How?"

"I'm getting my own paper."

"With what?"

"My dad's guilt."

"Guilt is good. Let's go in here for coffee. I'm freezing my ass off."

Sage pours two mugs of self-serve and leads Rita to a booth. "Drink this," she orders.

"Will I shrink?"

Sage looks blank.

"*Alice* . . . ," says Rita. "*Drink me.*"

"You read that to me."

"Will I?"

"I don't think so. But you might get warm."

"I don't feel any cold," says Rita. "I don't feel any *anything.*"

"How many hours have you been awake?"

"I haven't slept since we got back. I've been doing crosswords."

"This guilt . . . " says Sage, pouring sugar.

"It takes the form of cold, hard, cash."

"I've always liked that about him," says Sage, smiling.

Rita smiles too, but only with her lips. "I'm going back. Home."

"Home," Sage repeats.

"Home," says Rita firmly.

"You'll *die* there."

"He's going to set me up in business, and he's giving me the house. I can sell it and buy another. I can rent it out. Or I can live in it myself. Whatever I want."

"What *do* you want?"

"I have to go back. There's some kind of unfinished business there."

"Eddie?"

"Not just him. Something else. Something I have to do. I can't quite put my finger on it yet."

She packs up the Volvo again.

Sage isn't coming this time. It's just as well; there's no room for her. This time.

Rita doesn't have a lot of stuff. She's not a gatherer of *things.*

Everything she owns fits neatly into the Volvo.

***Choice* is** where you take it.

26

Sage studies hard for finals. She has to if she wants to pass.

I've been fucking around all year. It's time to get real.

Someone has to take care of her mother's things and, as it turns out, that someone is Rita. Neither her father nor Raymond want to do it. Raymond's girlfriend Tina does, but Rita won't allow it. *She's not even blood.*

Tina is constantly at her door, asking for coffee, wanting to chat.

Rita starts closing the blinds, not answering the door. Changes all the locks and has new keys made.

She packs up her mother's things. Clothing in bags for charity, stacks of homemaker's magazines for recycling. Takes the dusty trinket clutter from the bookshelves and uses the space for her own books.

Tina catches her one afternoon beating house rugs in the back yard. "*Here* you are!" she says brightly. "It looks like you've been busy. I've been dropping by, but you're never here."

"I was just about to take a break."

Tina follows her into the house. "It sure is cold."

Rita bumps into her with the pitcher from the fridge. "Sorry," she says.

"You must eat like a bird. You got no food in there."

Rita slams the fridge door. "Pull up a chair."

Tina sits while Rita gets glasses, an ashtray, and her cigarettes. "Why are you here?" she asks finally.

"I was just passing by, and I thought *maybe Rita's lonely. Maybe she needs a little company.* So, here I am. I get so bored during the day when Ray's at work. There's nothing to do."

"Why don't you get a job?"

"Ray's so old-fashioned. *No wife of mine is going to work,* he says. *I'm the breadwinner,* he says. *I wear the pants in this family.*"

"That Raymond!" Rita says with what she hopes might pass as fond affection.

"He's the man, alright. But he doesn't like me coming here. He says you'll put *ideas* into my head."

"Ideas?"

"He says you're *too radical.* He says you think *women should rule the world.*"

"That's not a bad idea."

"He sure didn't like that pallbearer business."

"Did *you* think there was something wrong about it?"

Tina shakes her head.

"Not me," she says. "But lots of people around here agree with Raymond, that *ladies should stay in their place.*"

"Which is?"

"You know . . . having babies. Cooking, cleaning, laundry. Looking after your man."

"Ah," Rita says. "Well, I'm never going to have kids, so that lets me off the hook."

"Oh, I'm so sorry. I didn't know you couldn't have kids."

"It's not that I can't. I won't. By choice."

"Well . . . " says Tina heavily. "I'm due in October."

"You're pregnant now?"

"Oh, don't worry, I won't show till after the wedding. It'll just happen a little early, that's all."

"Shit," Rita says, stubbing out her cigarette.

Keep anything of hers you want, Rita's father says.

So she keeps the crystal unicorn collection and her mother's boxes of letters.

But when she asks him what he wants, he says *Nothing*. So do Raymond and Dan.

She doesn't ask Timmy, but sets aside a few things to give to him when he's older.

The ghosts have gone, and she finally feels alone in the big house.

In the evenings she works out her business budget.

The town shuts down around eight at night and comes to life again around eight each morning, except on Sundays.

She takes long walks late at night, stares at dark houses, at television screens winking through drapes, and breathes the crisp night air.

Once, when she passes the fourplex where Raymond and Tina live, she sees Tina. Out on the side steps. Crying into her palms.

She lightens her step, hurries by.

Stay out of it, warns the voice in Rita's brain.

She sees Raymond and Tina at Economy Foods in the new strip-mall off Main Street. Tina pushing the grocery cart while Raymond checks prices and makes decisions.

Rita follows them.

Tina leans heavily against the cart handle. Unsteady, head bowed, hair in her face.

Rita catches up.

"Oh, hi!" she says to Tina. "I haven't seen you around for a while."

"She's been busy," says Raymond curtly. "Why are *you* here?"

"Just picking up a few things."

Then Tina sweeps her hair straight back in a single, defiant motion and Rita recognizes the tight shiny skin around her right eye.

"Why don't you come by for coffee one day?" she asks.

"Teen's real busy these days." Raymond lays his muscled forearm around her shoulder. "The wedding's next month."

"Maybe I could help," Rita says brightly. "I've never done that sort of thing before, but I could learn."

"Teen's sisters have it under control."

"Well, if there's anything I can do . . . "

Tina nods. "Thanks Rita. I'll let you know."

Raymond pushes the small of her back with his angular hand. "We better get a move-on. There's lots to do."

Now she makes a point of passing the fourplex during her night walks.

Most of the time, blinds are pulled tightly down over the windows so nothing escapes.

Once the blinds are open wide enough for Rita to see blurred shadows in front of a television, but that's all she can see no matter how much she strains.

Shuttered windows, bolted metal, can't see *outside*.

Provides her paints, easel, studio, all she could possibly need for one lifetime.

Only there is nothing to *see*.

Just what's inside, but not enough blacks and reds to fill the canvas for that vision.

Just what's *inside* and no amount of paint could ever fill the canvas of this vision.

Raw naked self is in his eyes when he cradles her at night. But by day he is all rage.

She locks herself inside their bathroom while he taunts her through the hollow wood.

Paint a pretty picture with your blood, Princess.

His song becomes a chant; over and over and over again he sings it.

She has shrunk into the shower curtain, wrapped herself inside the purple plastic, matching the towels on the bars, matching the bathmat, matching the tiny purple footprints stuck to the tub to prevent falling. Covers her ears with hands that tremble.

She cannot see Real World outside. He has bolted steel plates over all the windows in the house. No world exists for her now except this house. This door. These walls.

She knows he can easily break the lock, he has done it before.

But this time, he doesn't.

It must be time for him to go to work.

27

"We've been jerkin' around this planet for too long. That's why it's still so fuckin' cold."

"I'm edgy. This town is just too quiet."

"There's slime under all those rocks."

"These kids we went to school with!"

"What kids?"

"All of them. They're *parents*."

"It hasn't been nine months yet, has it?"

"Come back," Rita begs. "I need some company."

"I'm making good money here now."

"Waitress jobs are a dime a dozen."

"Farmers don't tip."

"I think Raymond's beating Tina. Nothing I can prove, just a hunch."

"He's scum," says Sage.

"He's my brother."

"He's still scum."

"I know."

"They're not married yet, are they? Tell her to get out of it."

"She's pregnant."

"Oh fuck."

"And she's *meek*. Like all the women in town."

"No wonder you're going crazy."

"There's always old Miss Riley who used to run the Post Office," Rita says. "She's queer as a three dollar bill."

"She's way too old for you."

"Please come home."

Rita asks people what they think of having a town paper.

The school custodian Gus, who has an opinion on everything. "There did used to be a weekly here," he says. "But I think the owners decided this town wasn't big enough to support it."

"Do you think we need one?"

"It's a good way to find things out. Gossip, want ads, advice columns. Who did what to whom. And you're the one to run it. You're the best goddamn editor the *Gazette* ever had."

"I'm going to."

"Go for it," says Gus.

"I'm calling it *RagTime*. And no one — not the school board, not the fucking churches, not the business*men* — can tell me what I can, or cannot, write about."

"What they *can* do," says Eddie, "is not buy your paper. Or not advertise. Kill you that way."

"I'm tired of your never-ending Devil's Advocate," Rita snaps. "Give me something I can use."

"I want to work for you," says Eddie. "So bad, I can taste it."

"You're on!" says Rita.

"I'm staying. I'm going to work for the new paper Rita's starting."

"Stop wetting yourself over this broad and get on with your life. Babes are a dime a dozen where you're going. Working for a *girl*. Christ!"

Eddie stares at him for a long while, this father in his undershirt, hairy chest and arms, a beer can between his meaty thighs. There's something so tight lodged in his throat, he can't swallow it back. Maybe he should just *spit it out*. But then his heart starts thumping through his ears and he can't hear himself think anymore. Can't see anymore.

"I'm going out," he says over the banging in his head.

"At least lumber is *man's work*," his dad hollers after him.

Eddie slams the door. Starts running.

"I've decided to come back for summer. With one condition," says Sage.

"Condition for *me*?"

"No sex."

"At all?" asks Rita. "Or just not with me?"

"Will you help with the flowers for the wedding?"

"What exactly does that mean?"

"Drive me to the florist."

"Sure," says Rita. "No problem."

"You look exhausted."

"I've got no energy," says Tina. "My mom's like this too, when she's pregnant. It runs in the family. We get anaemic."

"Is Raymond taking care of you?" asks Rita, eyes on the road.

Tina laughs dead.

Rita stops the car.

"I've got to ask," she says, staring through the windshield, "does my brother hit you?"

"What makes you think that?"

"A feeling. The way you look. The way he is."

"How do I look?"

"Like you've been damaged. I've been there. I know what it's like."

"Some guy punched *you* out?"

"Woman. But it doesn't make any difference."

"We should get going. I've got a lot to do."

Rita starts the car again.

"You don't have to tell me. But remember, if you ever need help, I'm here."

Rita paces her house top to bottom.

Opens the laundry room door and a quick fear memory shoots up her spine.

There are still some ghosts left in this house after all.

They're all coming from the city for Raymond's wedding. Her father, Nancy, Dan, and Timmy.

"Don't trouble yourself about the house," Nancy says. "We're staying at the motel."

"Not even Timmy?"

"We'll be out of your hair. Don't worry, it'll be fine this way."

"She's deliberately keeping him away," Rita tells Sage. "I'm his sister. She's just some tramp my father happened to pick up."

Sage sighs. "Your family is one winning combination!"

"I think my mother was holding us together."

"The glue wasn't strong enough. And it was only for appearances."

"It was better than this nothing."

"Well, *they're* all together."

"I don't like your no-sex condition," Rita complains.

"You agreed."

"Under pressure. It wouldn't hold up in court."

"Lucky we're not in court," grins Sage.

Now Sage walks at night with Rita. Every night they pass the fourplex. Every night Rita tries to spy through their blinds.

"He's hiding something."

"They're probably screwing in their living room. Like any normal couple. In front of the television."

"Is that really normal?"

"How the fuck should I know," Sage snorts, "what *normal* is. That's just what everyone says about half of North America being conceived during the *Tonight Show*."

"Should I ask them over for dinner?"

"Who?"

"My family. Maybe I'd get to see Timmy then."

"Sounds good to me. There's Lorraine, waiting up. See you tomorrow."

Sage kisses the air beside Rita's face.

"Good-night," says Rita glumly.

And walks on through her knee-deep drift of thought.

"Daddy," Rita says. "I want to talk to you. Alone."

"There's nothing you can't say to Nancy too," her father says.

"Please."

"We'll meet you at the coffee shop later," he says. "After we get Timmy to bed."

"I'll be there at nine-thirty."

Rita orders coffee, and waits until nine-fifty before Nancy and her father show up.

"Timmy had a hard time getting to sleep," Nancy says briskly. "In a strange bed."

"He could've had his own bed."

Nancy raises her eyebrows at Rita's father. He clears his throat.

A waitress pours coffee and passes menus.

"We'll each have a slice of your delightful chocolate cake," her father says, handing the menus back.

The waitress smiles shyly and scampers off.

"It looks like she remembers you," says Nancy.

"Jealous?" he teases.

Nancy glances at Rita, watching. "What's this meeting about?" she asks.

"There's a couple of things I wanted to talk to *my father* about."

"Such as?"

"Raymond and Tina," says Rita. "And Timmy."

The waitress returns with the cake, sets it down. "Enjoy," she says.

Rita's father winks at her.

"Let's start with Raymond," says Nancy.

"I think he's beating on Tina. You should talk to him, Dad."

Her father frowns and sets down his fork. "That's a serious accusation. I hope you have good reason for it."

"I've seen Tina with bruises. She seems scared and she avoids me. I've seen the way Raymond treats her."

"Avoids you," Nancy repeats.

"Yeah. He told her I'd put ideas in her head. You know, dangerous radical stuff like *you have the right not to get beat up*."

"Maybe she simply doesn't want to be seen with you," says Nancy. "Because of what you are."

"Honey," says Rita's father gently. "Don't start."

"What I am."

"A lesbian," Nancy says delicately. "Tina seems like a nice, normal girl."

"I'm not doing anything with Tina, for crissakes! Will you talk to Raymond, Daddy?"

"Okay, okay. Now, what about Timmy?"

"I just wondered . . . " Rita's father is finishing his cake, but Nancy is watching Rita's mouth. "It seems like you don't want him to see me anymore."

"Not at all," her father says. "Where would you get that idea?"

"When I call, she won't let me talk to him. She won't let him stay with me. You've been here for a whole day, and I still haven't seen him."

"Rita," Nancy interrupts, "you're over-reacting. We've been trying to get Timmy through a difficult adjustment period. His mother has just died, for heaven's sake, and his whole world has been turned upside down."

"Isn't that all the more reason for some consistency? He's known me his whole life."

"Your father and I think it's better for Timmy not to dwell on the past. For the time-being, at least."

"Or maybe it's because I'm lesbian." Rita leans forward. "Maybe you're scared it'll rub off on him."

"We don't think," Nancy says, pursing her lips primly, "that you are his best choice for companionship. Not an ideal role model."

"So that's it, then." Rita shoves her plate across to her father. "Maybe you want this too," she says. "I have to leave now."

Rita sees Timmy on the wedding day, just before the ceremony begins. He's wearing a white suit with a turquoise cummerbund, and he's seated beside Nancy.

Nancy slicks down the little curly cowlick behind Rita's brother's left ear with her manicured fingertip.

Nancy's turquoise suit matches Timmy's cummerbund.

Blonde Nancy looks stunning in turquoise.

Rita's father's blonde head high beside Timmy, and Dan beside him. They look like a natural family.

The wedding party is dressed in turquoise and white.

The flowers in the church building are turquoise and white.

Rita is wearing red.

She waits for the preacher to ask if *anyone present objects* but he leaves it out.

Did they request that, or don't they ask that question anymore?

"Did you talk to Raymond like you promised?" Rita whispers to her father after the ceremony.

"Of course," he says, making eye contact with old acquaintances over her head.

"And?"

"Excuse me." Rita's father brushes her hand from his arm. "I have to go chat with Jim. We'll talk later."

"Why do you hate me so much?"

"It isn't you, exactly."

"What exactly is it, then?" Rita adds boiling water to the teapot, and Nancy lights a long cigarette.

"I'm only here because your father suggested it."

"I want some answers."

"I can't even imagine!" Nancy skims honey onto a teaspoon and shudders. "The thought of women. Together."

"Do you even like sex?"

"I enjoy sex with the right man. But I think what you do is sick."

"Maybe you're the sick one."

"You twist everything that's normal."

"What I do is as normal as anything else. And it doesn't hurt *you*."

"It's unnatural."

"Try thinking about it sometime. Maybe coming in another woman's mouth. Touching her breasts, her touching yours . . . "

Nancy makes a gagging sound, scrapes her chair further from Rita's.

"I want to see my brother."

Nancy slips the ivory trench coat over her shoulders, fans her hair carefully out over the upturned collar. "Fine. If it'll keep you happy."

"That's settled then."

"I'm only agreeing to this because of your father. Above all else, your father wants to *keep you happy*."

28

Lurking dragons behind every door. In every bar. In the office where she works. Inside her head. Being Dragon-Slayer Queen didn't work.

There isn't anyone left on the east coast who she hasn't fucked.

And writing the mystery doesn't solve it.

Who the hell am I?

Urgently Seeking Katie *Winthrop, or anyone knowing her whereabouts.*

She runs the ad in every major daily newspaper across the country.

It costs her an arm and a leg.

No one else will tell her what she needs to know.

In her windowless prison, Princess waters plants that do not require sunlight for their survival. Brushes velvety leaves to her skin for some tenderness.

This life she carries inside will be her secret only for a while.

Within her own sallow skin, and in her whispers to the plants that do not require sun, she wills the fetus to grow strong. She thinks she would trade her *everything* for it but her *everything,* she knows, is *nothing at all.*

What he discovers, he ends.

Good thing for you, he says, *I know what I am doing and how to do it right. Lucky for you,* he says, *you don't have to be butchered by some quack. Fortunately,* he says, *you will never have to be a mother. Aren't we lucky?* he says and laughs. *Aren't you lucky? You and I can have time for our careers. For each other.*

What career? she asks, foolish from the oxygen he feeds her. And she laughs too.

Oh, I wouldn't, he warns her, *laugh. Laughing,* he says, *would not be wise for you to do right now.*

His voice gets rough at the edges and she listens up. Gets wise. No laughter now, while he is busy eliminating useless tissue with a scalpel.

Okay, she says, *it's this oxygen you've been feeding me. You know, I get woozy, a little crazy. I'm sorry. There will be no more laughter.*

She sits because he allows it, and watches red bubbling from her womb.

Wishes she could capture this with paint. A still-life of fetus bubble.

If I tied your tubes, we wouldn't have this mess to deal with all the time, he offers.

She stays silent, holds her breath.

This Doctor has patiently explained to her how he would accomplish sterilization. Without anaesthetic. Has done his research.

We could just remove the entire mess, he said. *Snip off the clitoris, you'd never miss it. A bit of blood, no big deal. Or I could take out one tube at a time. But that's piecework. Take out the whole bunch all at once, that's the way to go. You could be conscious, watch the whole thing.*

So she waits, lips shut tight, watching blood bubbles like lava escaping.

Baby, she whispers later, *I am so sorry. So very sorry.*

Touches the mossy leaves of her night-time plants against her skin, and waits for this new pain to settle to the back inside.

She worries when he's late.

Is he dead?

What would happen to her then is a mystery.

She could not access the security system the Doctor has had installed to keep her safe.

Night would turn into day, would turn into night, into day and night, and she would never know.

His family might come sometime to divide the spoils, find her there, and release her.

What if he's dead?

Her jailer crawls into bed, grunts, and rolls over.

Rolls over dead, asleep, snoring.

When he bleeds, maybe that will be enough.

Since he can no longer use his Leader, he uses what he can.

Bottle, jagged broken edges.

Metal pipe.

Umbrella.

Cleans her out with acid enemas.

There is nothing he doesn't use against her.

KTL builds a plan like a painting.

First, the wash. Then the blocking. Next, colour.

Her brush strokes bold.

There is nothing more to lose.

She uses the only language left they both understand.

Coward! she says. *Crawl.*

I'll never touch you again, he begs. *I'll release you. I promise.*

Promise? she asks, cold as silver.

He thinks *promise* is the magic charm but every time he says it, she shuts off more inside.

This is difficult for me, she says. *By nature, I am not angry,* she says. *Not that you would know, having raised this fear in me.*

His body pain makes him grunt.

I know how thirsty you get, she says. *I'll be right back.*

Fridge light flickers on the beer stored there. *For him. For his pleasure.*

Beer? she asks, uncaps, begins to pour. *Whiskey would be better, I think.*

The golden liquid puddles into the raw ridges she has left on his skin.

It will keep away infection, as you always say, she says. *Your wisdom.*

He is quiet, for a change.

KTL steps back from his crumpled body.

More? she asks, politely.

It seems like every lunatic in the country reads the personal columns.

Pearce's first full-length murder mystery is being published.

She's signed the contract. *The Amorous Assassin* has gone to print.

"Don't quit your day job yet," the publisher tells her. "Strong female leads are hard to sell. We don't know how this'll go."

She gives notice to Larry.

"I'm quitting. I'm going to college."

"How will we ever replace you?" he asks, staring hard at her blouse.

"You won't."

"You'll get too smart for us."

"I already am."

Pearce laughs.

29

KTL calls the police.

There's a dead man here, she says. *But you'll have to break in. I've been locked up for years.*

Sage perches on the edge of Rita's desk in her new office, playing with a stack of floppy disks.

"What's the first issue going to be about?"

"Leave those alone," snaps Rita.

"Don't you have anything better to do than come here and pester us?" Eddie asks. "Why don't you get a job or something?"

"Rags is the biggest employer in town now. And she won't hire me."

"You have no skills. You can't even type."

"I'll sell subscriptions door-to-door. Give me a chance."

"It's incredible how news piles up. Everyone's calling us with bits and pieces. It's amazing. One minute there's no newspaper, so there's no news. Next minute there's way too much."

"All you've got is an editor and one reporter. You'll never manage it all," says Sage. "I can answer the phones and write stuff down."

"There's an election for town council," Eddie says. "The news is that no one's running for mayor."

"Old Harry's retiring?"

"Yeah, finally," says Rita. "But nobody else wants it."

"There's a job for you," Eddie says. "Run for mayor."

"What does a mayor do?"

"Dick-all. Harry had time to be mayor and run a mail-order business."

"What do you need to qualify?"

Sage kicks her heels against Rita's new desk.

"You're scuffing up my finish," Rita complains.

"Harry didn't even graduate from High School," Eddie says, flipping through a bunch of papers on his desk. "I think all you have to do is declare your candidacy."

"What does it pay?"

"More than waitressing."

"But you need to have a prick," says Rita. "There's never been a woman mayor, and there never will be. Not here."

"Wanna bet?" crows Sage.

Eddie has a hard-on.

At his desk in the *RagTime* office, watching Rita fiddle with her new Macintosh.

Soft, ragged blue jeans, crisp white shirt, blue denim jacket; she looks fantastic.

Eddie couldn't stand up now to save his life.

"Come on, Maw," coaxes Sage.

"Where on earth did you get this idea? I've been a secretary all my life. It's the only thing I know."

"You've been running that place for years and you know it. Everybody does. You're a fuckin' natural. And I'll be your campaign manager. I need the work."

FIRST WOMAN THROWS HAT
INTO MAYORAL RING

screams Rita's first headline.

The deadline passes. Sage is ecstatic and Rita's getting great copy.

Three weeks and two more issues of *RagTime*.

"Fuckin' Lorraine knows *everything*," Sage brags.

"You have to watch that mouth of yours," says Eddie. "Once she's mayor, you can't be *fucking this* and *fucking that*. Maybe nobody else wants the job, but that won't stop them from crucifying her."

The two of them, like puppies, each with her own new squeak toy.

He's tired of watching Sage jerk Rita's chain. Tired of her being in their office all the time. Tired of sharing Rita.

I had her all to myself. We could've been lovers by fall.

Tina pounds on Rita's door late one night.

"Let me stay here," she begs. "He's going to kill me."

"We're going to the city, and I'm buying us some decent suits. You cannot manage my campaign dressed like that."

Sage stares at her reflection in the hall mirror.

"What the hell's wrong with this?"

"It's not presentable," Lorraine says firmly. "Ripped shorts and a halter are not mayoral."

"You don't have money for suits."

"Watch me!"

"What about Daddy?"

"He's on his own. I've been keeping my money."

Sage flings her arms around her mother. "Let's go buy us some fucking suits!"

Eddie's picking at his fingernails when Rita comes in.

"On the street," he says, "they're saying she's *just a woman*."

"They're also saying," says Rita, "that she's been running council all these years. People respect Lorraine around here."

"She managed to get respect by keeping to herself even though she worked. And because she did it to support her kid and that no-good husband of hers," says Eddie. "I sure hope Sage doesn't go messing it up for her."

"She won't."

"You love her. That's why you don't see what everyone else sees."

"She might surprise us, Eddie. Give her a chance."

"At least it's only a few years until the next election. Maybe she can manage to keep her nose clean that long."

Sage models her new suits for them in the *RagTime* office.

"I love that red one!" says Rita.

"A suit won't change anything," Eddie mutters.

Rita glares.

"Don't you have a story to dig out? What am I paying you for, anyway?"

Raymond breaks into Rita's house, and drags Tina back to the fourplex with him.

You belong to me now cunt, he tells her.

30

Only quiet now, both in and outside of KTL's brain.

She believes she has slept.

She believes her heavy eyes have closed and her busy mouth has stopped twisting itself around its endless litany for once, for a time.

She has slept, she believes, without sound.

Even her relentless wind has stopped.

She awakens, looks at her two hands. Holds them up in front of her two eyes.

Sees their true colour. *Pink.*

Her true nail colour is *white.*

The tips of her true nails are jagged from where she chews on them to stop the wordfall from her mouth.

What do I do now? she wonders.

A day for wonderment, for awe.

KTL grasps this wondrous day with her good two hands *pink* and her good two eyes *blue.*

What do I do now?

She pulls down the blanket *grey* which covers her body.

Sees her good two breasts, her one slightly protruding belly with its fuzzy navel, her one good pelvis, her two good strong thighs and her two good knees, her two good feet.

It is a good-body day.

Her belly sags slightly when she sits.

This body is growing old while this brain stays in childhood.

This older body betrays that young girl who raised the wind for protection.

Flesh of flesh, bone of bone, blood of blood.

Perhaps that wind will disappear for good if she stops thinking, leave her at last to watch this good body thicken and set.

Her easel is packed in its leather satchel by the door, the one possession she kept all this time just for herself.

Maybe she will go out, find something to paint onto canvas. By the riverbank maybe, or by the park.

KTL stretches one of her two good bare feet, then the other.

Touches the first, then the second, to the cold floor. Feels the cold and knows this is good.

Gingerly, she sets weight on those two good feet, and she does not fall.

She takes her own weight full, standing.

Takes her full, standing weight to the bathroom behind the bed which is in her sitting room, the room in which she sits.

Pees sitting, her two good feet in front where she can keep her two eyes on them.

Takes them and her full-weight body into the shower stall, runs steamy water all over it.

Lathers in shampoo, soap, rinses.

Dries her one good body with a *pink* towel.

Brushes the hair, *some grey*, with the *brown* hairbrush.

Sprinkles on talcum, *white*.

Choosing clothes, *black* denims, *white* shirt, *red* belt, *black* socks, *black* sneakers, she feels *hunger*.

This is a sensational day.

KTL laughs aloud.

On Election Day, Mrs. Winthrop goes to the polling station to spoil her ballot.

This election is a farce, she thinks.

But she speaks to no one.

Her voice has rusted away.

On Election Day, Tina miscarries her baby.

Raymond did this, she tells Rita. *It's because he hit me.*

Will you tell the cops now?

Yeah, Tina says finally.

Election Day.

Mother and daughter go together to the polls.

Eddie shoots their photograph for the newspaper.

"Who did you vote for?" he asks Lorraine while he takes the picture.

Lorraine treats Sage to dinner.

"To my mom the mayor!" says Sage, raising her glass.

"I'm getting worried," Lorraine says.

"You'll be fine, Maw."

Rita joins them later, for dessert.

"Come home with me," she whispers when Lorraine leaves to pay their bill.

"Time to get home to bed," says Lorraine. "Tomorrow's the big day."

"I'm going back to Rita's," says Sage. "Don't wait up."

Rita memorizes Sage's skin with her fingertips. Drawing out smooth lines, pressing at all her indentations.

"I'll never love anyone else," she says.

"You were in love with Charlotte. And Susan. And I don't know who all else."

"Not like this."

"But it never works for us together."

Rita runs her finger along Sage's lips.

"Why," asks Sage, crushing her hand against Rita's gentle fingers, "does it feel like we're saying *goodbye*?"

When Rita bounds into the office the next morning, Eddie is already there, contemplating his typewriter.

"You'll have to learn to use the computer. Typing is passé," she says, mussing his hair when she passes.

Being touched by Rita.

"That old lady Winthrop died yesterday," he says. "They found her outside her house. She just went out to vote, got home, dropped dead."

"Winthrop?"

"Sage's old friend Pearce? Her grandma."

"Shit!"

"They're saying she had a bundle squirrelled away. The lawyers are looking for the granddaughter."

"If there's something in it for her, they'll find her. No problem."

"What have you got against her?"

"It's a long story."

"I'd bet it's got something to do with Sage," Eddie says grimly.

"You'd win," Rita snaps.

Harry's assistant Etta is helping Sage clean out his office for Lorraine.

"That old guy sure knew how to hoard," says Etta. "Look at all this shit."

"Anal-retentive. What's in there, anyway?"

"Post-its, glue sticks, staples, stuff like that. That old fool was using our money for years to support that mail order business of his."

"Save what you think we can use."

Etta hands her three packages of cotton swabs.

"Here, clean out your ears or something," she says. "It'll be like a breath of fresh air for me to work for your mother."

Sage is staring through the window overlooking Main Street.

Presses her nose flat against the pane and feels five years old again. *In Mom's office.* One flattened nose.

"Do we want these staplers? There's fifty of them in here, all brand-new. All the same."

"I wonder if there's receipts. What the fuck are we going to do with fifty brand-new, all-the-same staplers?"

Etta sits back on stockinged heels and squints at Sage, gilt-framed by sun.

"Too bad about that old lady Winthrop."

Sage snaps back.

"Too bad what?"

"How she died."

"She died?"

"Heart attack, they think. The neighbour found her lying outside her house with the key in her hand. She must've been coming back from voting. You know, she wasn't even all that old."

"I wonder if Pearce will come back."

"That granddaughter of hers? They'll be trying to find her. *Someone* gets her fortune."

"Pearce," says Sage softly.

"I guess, if she's still alive. That poor miserable old lady. Lost everything. First her husband, then her daughter. And then there was all that talk."

"Are they dead?"

"No one really knows. Talk was that the husband and the daughter . . . well, best to let those sleeping dogs lie."

Sage's heart is beating so hard she thinks she may throw up.

A grey-eyed baby has formed her shape inside KTL's brain.

She can't twist it away, and she can't force it to talk.

KTL packs her easel and her paints and a few clothes into her green satchel.

Walks with the satchel to the bus depot.

Buys a ticket.

Waits at the water fountain for the loudspeaker to tell her it's time to board.

Joins the other passengers in line outside the silver Greyhound.

You can leave your bag, ma'am, the man in the blue uniform tells her when he punches her ticket.

KTL clutches the satchel tightly, away from his outstretched hand.

You can't have it, she says inside her head.

The man in the uniform grimaces, motions her up the steps with a jerk and a nod.

That grey-eyed baby stares and stares at KTL as she finds her seat at the back where they will be safer, away from Real World prying eyes and ears.

Keeps staring at her while the engine starts, and while the driver navigates the bus through city streets.

Downtown buildings disappear, are replaced with smaller strip malls, then motels, then quiet residences, and then by the open prairie.

Not much Real World here.

Grain elevators and occasional farm yards, and lines and lines of power coursing across the wide, white sky.

It's cold in this bus despite the bold summer sun out there.

KTL wraps her fuzzy woollen sweater around her shoulders, tucks her knees up to her chin, and keeps looking out.

The grey-eyed baby looks out too.

There, there, croons KTL but this baby will not talk.

We'll get there eventually, says KTL. *You don't have to talk. I think I understand.*

31

TELEGRAM
PEARCE NAVIA WINTHROP: TO NOTIFY NEXT-OF-KIN.
YOUR GRANDMOTHER MRS. ESTHER WINTHROP
SUDDENLY DECEASED. REQUEST YOU NOTIFY US AT ONCE
AS TO DESIRED ARRANGEMENTS.
BRICKLY & BRACKETT
ATTORNEYS AT LAW

"Pearce is coming."

"Who said?"

"Eddie called the lawyers to check."

Sage holds her eyes bold, full on Rita.

"What did they say?"

Rita shifts in her chair.

"They said they sent her a telegram, and she called."

"Did she say she was coming?"

"Sage . . . "

"Did she?"

"Yeah. Yeah, she said."

"Oh man! Oh-fucking-man. Pearce is coming, oh-man-oh-fucking-man!"

"You'll fall in love with her all over again. Then she'll leave and break your heart."

Five a.m.

Time to be crawling out from under whatever body is in her bed. Pouring coffee, vodka, maybe sucking reefer. Lights off, staring at nothing. Considering dragons. Something always *out there*, somewhere, beyond the horizon, beyond her grasp.

Five o'clock.

But this morning she is flying. Back.

Plane hits a hard pocket. Jerks and rears like some spooked pony.

It's five-o-three.

Sage puts on her favourite new suit, the red one, to go to the bus depot. To wait.

She guzzles from the water fountain and checks her make-up a hundred times in the reflective window.

The last bus of the day is due in twelve minutes.

Maybe with Pearce.

Nine more minutes.

But the only passenger getting off is a woman in a moss green dress, clutching a satchel tightly against her hip.

Sage shrugs at a vague and nagging memory.

"Is there anyone else getting off?" she asks the driver, out for a smoke.

"Nope. Not at this stop."

"When's the next one coming in from the city?"

"Tomorrow at five-thirty."

He grinds the cigarette under his boot.

"Maybe I'll see you then."

"Someone special you're expecting? Boyfriend?"

"Special," says Sage.

The woman with the satchel has disappeared.

This is where I lived, KTL tells her grey-eyed baby. *It's where you lived too. We both lived here, you and I, for some time. She keeps the key here, under the mat. See?*

The slate-faced baby is still silent.

I do understand, KTL tells her. *You were born to fear. Let's put it away now.*

Pearce takes the bus from the city.

Her roots are further out. Along the highway. Where this bus is taking her.

Daddy's home *little Princess.*

KTL shakes that old monster back and he retreats, just as she has trained him to do.

There is room inside for only so many voices, and then no more.

And this baby now has her full attention.

She carries her green satchel to the never-used front room and sits down. To wait.

Pearce talks to herself as the Greyhound clicks out the miles.

I wonder if Sage still has that box I made her keep for me?

Patience, KTL tells the baby *is a virtue.*

We can wait.

We can out-wait them all.

32

"He forced himself on her."

"I thought it was supposed to have been a secret," says Sage. "I thought no one knew."

"I never found out what happened to her afterwards. I think she went crazy. No wonder, with a baby at fourteen, and that mean old woman who never forgave."

"I'm telling Pearce, if she does come back."

"No! I was the only one on Katie's side, and I've kept her secret. You may *not* betray her. Do you understand?"

"I can't promise that, Mom," says Sage quietly. "You know that. Pearce has the right to know."

"What the fuck are you doing here?" Sage barks.

"If you're going to hang around here for the next week, or till she gets here, I'm going to be here too," says Rita calmly.

"You've got a fucking paper to run."

"And you've got fucking business to attend to for Lorraine. What's your point?"

"I don't want you to be here when she comes."

"This is a public place."

"I'll get a fucking by-law."

"When's the next bus?"

"Five-fucking-thirty."

"Five-fucking-thirty it is then. Let's grab a coffee and a smoke while we wait."

"I can't. I'm too fucking tense."

"I sure do love what Pearce does to you. You're delightful company."

"You're being an asshole."

"Whatever," says Rita, lighting her cigarette.

She's almost here, KTL whispers to the baby by her side *I can feel it.*

Sage's mouth is dry as bone, but her hands are wet.

"It's her!" she whispers, grabbing Rita's hand.

"Pearce!" calls Rita.

The green-jeaned woman pauses.

"Pearce," Rita says again.

They are so close, they can nearly touch each other.

"I didn't expect anyone . . . " says the woman.

"This is *Sage*," Rita says, tugging Sage's hand. "Remember?"

"I was going to try to find you. You look so different."

"A big difference between thirteen and twenty," says Sage, finding her voice, "but I'd know *you* anywhere."

"Manma died."

"That's how we found out you'd be coming. This is Rita. She owns the newspaper."

"Sometimes things do change after all."

Behind them all, Eddie lurks.

This should be interesting. Things might turn around this summer after all.

Pearce slings her arm around Sage.

Rita stands stiff beside them. Rita stands there while Sage grabs Pearce's bag.

"Rita!" Eddie yells. "Rags! Over here!"

Rita turns, smiles. "Hi Eddie! I didn't see you over there."

Eddie's melting down inside. "Come with me for coffee. Have I got a story for you!"

"I didn't know it, but I've loved you," Sage says, "all this time."

"This is so hard," Pearce says, shifting on the park bench where late afternoon sun pours over her.

"Yeah."

"There's been a whole lifetime since then. A lot of things that happened. I can't make commitments. I don't seem to have it in me. Or love."

"Oh." Sage squints into sun.

"I still don't know who I am. I've been searching for Katie. Did you keep that box of stuff like you promised?"

"It's in Lorraine's house. I've never even looked at it."

"I trusted you," Pearce says. "I think I'll get it while I'm here."

"How long . . . "

"Long enough to sell that old house, tie up loose ends. Then I'm out of here. I'll be rid of it then. Free."

"Will you keep in touch this time?"

"I intend to go to school. I intend to write another book. I intend to figure out who the fuck I am."

"None of those includes me. I'll bet you won't even write."

"I'm sorry . . . I'm not whatever it is you want me to be."

Sage swallows something bitter. "Okay then. At least now I know."

"You can bury it."

"Yeah."

KTL's voice is tired. Not from use, but from the long silence.

I have a story, she says *and then you'll tell me yours.*

Pearce is locked tight on this woman.

Words, like paint.

The *brush* of a *tongue.*

Pretty pretty baby, *paint Daddy a picture,* says the man with the wide white smile.

And from the wind he raises, this grey-eyed baby born.

Give it to Mama. A replacement for *his* love; she wants it more than life.

Now get out whore, Mama says, *I never want to see you again. I owe you nothing.*

Daddy takes her to the city in his car, the red one with wings.

My little Princess, he sings.

Rests his face in the palms of his hands pressed against the steering wheel *I'll always love you* while he weeps sour tears into his hands *but I have to let you go now.*

Flesh of flesh, blood of blood, bone of bone.

That *loving* he gave her first ripped her apart.

Take good care of my baby, he tells the man.

You'll be in good hands Princess, he says, *this man's a Doctor.*

"I've been so confused, crippled almost," Pearce says.

I know. This baby told me.

"Will you stay with me now?"

No, but I'm leaving the baby with you, says KTL. *Her weight has been killing me.*

"What will I do with her?"

This is the most I can give, says KTL.

Rita knocks on the door of the big old Elm Street house. Again.

Pearce opens it, just a crack. "What do you want?"

"To talk . . . to you," Rita stammers. "Can I come in?"

"I don't think so."

"Is Sage with you?"

"Not Sage," Pearce whispers, glancing behind. "Someone else."

"Can we talk out here, then?"

"I'm right in the middle of something."

"Look. I know you never knew me at all, but I've known Sage for a long time. Forever. I sort of know you through her. Anyway, I've always wondered about something."

"What?"

"Did you ever find out about your parents?"

"Yes."

"Would you mind telling me?"

"Why?"

"Please," Rita begs. "I can't say why, but it's important."

"I've learned," Pearce says proudly, "that my mother was a Princess."

"Wow!" says Rita.

Pearce strides down the sidewalk, head held high.

Lorraine answers the door. "Come in. Sage said you were back."

"Is she home?"

"Sage!" Lorraine calls.

"This house is exactly the same. It even smells the same."

"Honey, look who's here!"

Sage shuffles, looks at her feet, then at Pearce. "You want your stuff, right?" she asks.

"Imagine! All this time!" beams Lorraine.

"You were my mother's only friend here," says Pearce. "I know about it now. Where's that box?"

"Upstairs," says Sage.

Lorraine watches them run up the stairs together, a couple of kids.

"You've still got the planets up there. I remember when you painted those."

"What are you going to do with this stuff now?"

"I think I'll start a fire," says Pearce.

Eddie slouches in his desk across from Rita who's hunched over her computer.

"Why aren't you working, Eddie?" she asks at last.

"Is that how long it takes for you to notice me?"

"Is this some kind of test?"

Eddie stands and stretches. "How long is it going to take for Winthrop to finish her affairs?"

"I don't know. Why?"

"Because, as long as she takes is as long as you'll be like this." Eddie opens the office door. "I'm going for coffee. Maybe dinner. Maybe breakfast. Let me know when you get back."

Sage walks to the bus depot with Pearce.

"Send me an autographed copy of your book," she says. "Write to me."

"I promise."

"I'll probably still be here. Or send it to Lorraine and she'll get it to me. Can I kiss you goodbye?"

"It'll be some scandal," says Pearce.

An old familiar feeling washes over Sage when they touch.

She blinks it away along with her tears.

"I'll always love you," she whispers.

Pearce laughs.

Then she vanishes into the bus.

Pearce holds her new grey-eyed baby close inside, rocking her with the rhythm of the bus.

Katie.

Eddie's father is working at his lumber store where Eddie goes to cut a spare set of keys to his new apartment.

"I'm moving out, Dad," he says. "I've taken enough."

"Pearce said she found out her mother was a *Princess,*" Rita says. "Did she tell you?"

"I don't know about that." Sage shrugs. "It never bothered me."

"I wonder how she found out."

"It's not your business. It never was. All I know is that I can get on with the rest of my life now."

"Everyone keeps talking about the *rest of their lives,*" says Rita. "What about the moment?"

"This *is* the fucking moment. This is *it*."

"Eddie wants me to marry him."

"Big surprise."

"He asked me twice."

"So?"

"So nothing. I'm just thinking about the *rest of my life*. Like everyone else around here."

"You've got a newspaper to run. That should take care of a few minutes."

KTL takes her satchel, steals out of town on the early morning Greyhound.

She's lighter without that baby.

Now that the Queen and the Princess and the Dragons have been buried.

That new grey-eyed woman will take good care of those treasures.

Enough of Real World.

This trip will be the last.

Lynnette (Dueck) D'anna's first book, *sing me no more*, was published by Press Gang Publishers in 1992. Her writing has been published in *CV2*, *Prairie Fire*, *Prism International*, *Poetry Canada* and *Grain*. D'anna is president of Prairie Fire Press Inc. She works in Winnipeg with Dance Collective and writes for *Interchange* magazine.

She has worked with Planned Parenthood, the Status of Women, and the Saskatoon AIDS Project. D'anna is an advocate for reproductive and other fundamental human rights. Her own abuse experiences have led her to an ongoing search for social and personal healing, and a few years ago she founded Post-Mennonite Survivors (PMS), a mutual support group for survivors of evangelical abuse.

In the real world, she has worked as a telephone operator, secretary, sales clerk, research assistant, hair stylist, and has dipped doubles at an ice cream stand.

D'anna is working on her third prose and first poetry manuscripts. She writes in a turret in Winnipeg and shares a home with her children, Abra and Moses, and their Foster Cat.